Homage to

Homage to a Firing Squad

Tariq Goddard

Homage to a Firing Squad

SCEPTRE

Typeset in Sabon by Palimpsest Book Production Limited,
Polmont, Stirlingshire
Printed and bound in Great Britain by
Mackays of Chatham PLC, Chatham, Kent

Hodder & Stoughton
A division of Hodder Headline
338 Euston Road
London NW1 3BH

To my mother and father

Prologue

'Thank you.'

When did I first say that to him? Why did it replace what had gone before and, having said it again, could there not have been something more appropriate to have said, something that would have betrayed how much I have improved since we last spoke, since I last spoke to him?

Don Rojo had always known that he had taken greater pains in revealing himself to the Lord than the Lord had in revealing Himself to Don Rojo, though never had he been more aware of it than now. Nor had he ever wished so hard for the Lord to give a little back and never, in the act of wishing, had he been so unsuccessful in concealing the anxiety that marked the space his wishes would arrive at.

Please . . . please speak up . . . please.

It was irrevocable. The two had become strangers and, with the weight of this admission lodged in his mind, Don Rojo began to plot his changing relations with God.

At first he had asked for nothing. Instead his mother, who would conduct prayers by the side of his bed, had acted as an intermediary between this world and the next, calling upon the Lord on behalf of the infant Rojo. The Lord, though largely indifferent, was still receptive enough to give the young Don-to-be enough space in which to reap the rewards of his mother's instruction. By the end of his first year at school he towered over his peers as their undisputed superior – triumphant in all respects and so confident as to not even notice the growth of his own powers. These powers, and the success they invited, corresponded to the requirements of age, so that childish gains were soon displaced by adolescent victories and these, in turn, gave way to a rapid ascendancy in politics.

So rapid, in fact, that when the time came for Carla Rojo to be reunited with her husband and her creator (the agent of her son's success) the whole city staged a day of mourning to honour their favourite matron. A grief so deeply felt that even on the floor of the National Parliament a minute's silence was observed as her son, leader of the opposition, lowered his head, with difficulty, and swore to continue the good work he had started. And though he did all he could to live by this oath, it became clear to all who indulged him that what was most valuable in Don Rojo died with his mother. Just like Pharaoh before him, he began to confuse his own role in his success and forgot how to say thank you.

Which was why now, after years free from humility and with little time left to live, Don Rojo was amused to find that 'thank you' was all that he was able to say, though, deep in the clearing where this sudden turnaround had happened, he could tell that it was too late to ask God for anything. Giving thanks was not the same as saying sorry. He tried, once again, to think of the last ordinary thing he had thought of before all this had begun, but his thoughts, like a tired army, had stopped obeying orders. The car was jerking up and down. They were moving off the road. He had run out of time.

Chapter One

He could feel something lighter than air pass over his face. Without moving he waited for it to happen again. If it did it would be good luck; if it did not it would be bad.

Don Rojo smiled complacently. He would lie there all night if he had to.

7.45 p.m. – the Montana Barracks

Twelve miles away a car pulled up behind the old army barracks, on the outskirts of town, and sounded its horn twice. Seconds passed and the horn was sounded again, this time with enough force for it to be heard over the noise of the running engine. A voice called out from one of the windows and, following its suggestion, the car reversed through a line of its own exhaust fumes and parked by the barracks forecourt. Largo, the driver of the car, stopped the engine, turned to the rear-view mirror and, checking that no one else could see, pulled a face. Like all the other faces he had pulled that day, this one failed to have the required effect and, acting quickly, he made it again, this time sucking his cheeks in like a fish. Instead of corresponding neatly with the reflection he anticipated, his face appeared in pain, like that of a man attempting to get up after a stroke.

He spat into his reflection, rolled the window up, and paused. Within seconds he had unwound the window and was once again staring into the mirror, unable to either believe or alter what he saw there: the same face he had had all day. His brooding was interrupted by the voice that had called out moments earlier.

'How long have you been waiting?'

'Not as long as all that.' The sound of his own voice reassured Largo since it displayed a quite misleading composure that the rest of him lacked.

'I didn't expect you to be this early.'

'I'm here now so hurry up,' Largo replied.

'I'm surprised that you even made it here . . . if what you got up to this morning is true,' the voice called back teasingly.

Largo shook his head and sighed, for the owner of the voice's benefit, and punched the rear-view mirror, for his own. It was a triumph of will over deformity for him to be able to drive a car at all. Standing at just under five foot without his shoes on, he was practically a dwarf. Driving a car was only possible with the aid of the metal stilt-like grafts his father had welded on to the soles of his shoes.

'Just get down here now,' he shouted at the top of his voice, hoping that this would at least make him sound like a dwarf who meant business.

Ali slammed shut the first-floor window he had

called from and, in seconds, could be heard thundering down the stairs.

Largo stretched over and opened the passenger door. For the first time he really was sure that today had been worse than the day before. 'You, Largo, are a coward,' she had said. 'You, Largo, are a coward,' he muttered beneath his breath. The insult had put an end to months of careful work. There had been no opportunity to say anything in his own defence. To have replied would have been impossible, knowing he was as ugly as he had come to accept he was. To be called a coward and only because he was ugly . . . convenient as this explanation was, he was still unable to fully believe in it. There was more wrong with him than just his face. Adjusting the cracked mirror, and addressing his own reflection, he narrowed his beady eyes and whispered, 'It would have been easy to kill the bitch.' Then, nodding solemnly, he readjusted the mirror and ran the stub of his thumb across his holster.

'In your own time, Largo.'

Largo sighed painfully. He would probably never be able to kill anyone and, as a consequence of this, he could already hear the world, and all the women in it, mocking him for this feminine vice. Lifting his tiny body up, so that he was virtually balanced against the steering wheel, Largo threw his foot down on the accelerator and moved the vehicle through its gears.

The car sped through the stretch of countryside that surrounded the barracks, past the burnt-out collective farms and the stockpiles of maize that lay uncollected outside their gates.

Largo peered up from the steering wheel. Above the bumpy road they were travelling along the sky was changing colour and small explosions of rain were starting to scatter across the windscreen of the car.

'That'll be another season's harvest wasted,' said Largo.

Next to him sat Ali, the boy they had collected from the barracks, and behind him the Captain and Josip. None of the men paid any attention to Largo's remark; instead they watched the rain gather strength and hammer the thick dust fields into mud.

Of the four only Largo, the driver of the car, had escaped being enlisted in the army, and this was only because his arms were too short to hold and fire a rifle. Nevertheless, Ali's mother had tailored a special uniform for him which he wore daily in his role as mascot for the local militia. This had been a great boost to Largo's confidence, since, despite the doubts of the last few hours, he rarely succumbed to self-pity unless he considered himself in the way he thought others saw him. The bottle-green uniform he now wore was the same colour as the Captain's, and since the Captain persisted in the civilian habit of slinging a leather coat over his service dress, Largo could appear, from a distance, as the highest-ranking officer in the car. This was not something Largo wished to voice openly, however, for fear of finding out that this was yet another honour his companions considered worthless.

Sensing his top lip tighten slightly, Largo felt another face possess him, one that would, in all probability, force words through his mouth.

'Okay, I'll be straight with you,' he heard himself blurt. 'You can say this is none of my business, but that doesn't mean that I'm not allowed an opinion.' Largo stretched his foot forward, and loosened the knot of the red bandanna tied around his throat. Somehow the piece of cloth seemed intent on asphyxiating him, not as a rope would, but like a glove pulled over his face.

'I think you may be able to grant me at least this,' he continued quickly but uneasily. 'I don't pretend to be one of these people who knows everything, but I have a handle on people. I *know* them, and it's because I do that I'm able to . . .' Largo paused; he was losing sight of what he was trying to say. 'Look, this is about Lucille Rojo, Rojo's daughter, you know?'

Behind him Largo could feel the Captain doing his best to feign deafness. He paused and wondered whether it was worth going on. Getting things off his chest was always difficult for him, which was why, when attempting to air his problems, he would often pretend to be talking about something else. If only he could gather the courage to *get to the point* . . .

A second's silence was followed by laughter, first from the Captain and then from all sides of the car bar Largo's, whose attention returned to the road. At moments like this experience had taught him that it was better to suffer in the midst of one's problems silently, as this would at least allow for a gap between the infliction of pain and the acceptance of any subsequent ridicule. As he cosseted himself from the others, Largo's thoughts returned automatically to the events at the barber's earlier that day. It was not hard for him to pare down, with the benefit of hindsight, his mistake, the mistake made in following everything she said and believing she would listen to him with the same attention. 'Oh, good, oh, well, that must be very nice for you,' was as reciprocal as she had been. Though now he thought about it, it became harder to remember just what it was he had said to her and the effect he hoped it would have. It was certainly something he was feeling steadily less pleased with, and he began to toy with the idea of blaming his limited vocabulary, the actual words he had used and his general lack of experience with girls.

'Are you going to tell me about the barber's or am I going to hear it from these two?' said Ali, his Moorish face alive with curiosity. His curiosity in Largo's story was, if he was honest, only of secondary interest. His real concern was with point-scoring and, as the youngest in the car and therefore, despite Largo's diminutive height, the most vulnerable, it was crucial for him to take his chances where he could. Shifting in his seat slightly, Ali willed Largo to say something, because despite what he had just said neither the Captain nor Josip could be relied on as foils in this sort of game, or as sources of gossip. The Captain because he considered himself above such things, and Josip through sheer country-boy indifference. 'Come on, Largo, stop pretending not to hear me . . .'

Largo's grip on the gear-stick tightened as the events of that morning became as real to him as they had when they first occurred. If anything, they grew more real, as reality was no longer there to interfere with them – now Lucille Rojo could lose her worldly reality and gain a new one. This new reality was one Largo could both invent and enjoy, one in which Lucille was easier to aim for, easier to fancy his chances with, in which it would be easier to lead this goddess to uses he would ultimately decide on . . . But this all still fell short of what he would have liked, to have been in the Captain's shoes and to have slept with her, to know what sort of fuck she was . . . and this, of course, reminded him of her worldly reality, and its great distance from his own. To place her in any context of his was useless; he could never reduce her to a size he would feel comfortable with. She was still too big for him to make the thought of her enter and re-enter his fantasies. Belching loudly as a way of countering this flight of fancy, he turned to thinking within the realms of the possible – to thinking of how long it would take to reach the Rojos' house from the dust tracks of the Tibidabo road.

'Come on, Largo, what did she say to you?'

'Leave it alone, and leave him alone, Ali,' the Captain said slowly. Hearing Largo mention Lucille Rojo had upset the Captain, who would rather not have been reminded of her at all. He squeezed the bicycle clip he wore on his shoulder. Did she still have hers or had she lost it, or perhaps thrown it away? It was difficult to resist improving on the last report he had heard of her, and as difficult to prevent this report from destroying one of his favourite conceptions. This particular conception being one in which each report he heard would indicate how much more suited to each other they were now, rather than remind him of how ill suited they were when they had first met. As it was, the days since he had seen her last had been characterised by false purpose, baseless dream creation and unrewarded patience. A lot of effort on his part and very little on hers, he felt.

'What the hell do we want to go down the Tibidabo road for anyway?' asked Ali impatiently, tugging at the sides of his seat like a child in need of the toilet. 'The view's crap, the track's shit and there are faster ways of getting to the Rojo hacienda . . .'

'You'll know by the time we get there,' the Captain replied, unsure of whether he was being guarded or unnecessarily deceptive. He disliked secrets for secrets' sake. Anything cloak-and-dagger smacked of affectation. Nor did he like having to be short with his men as neither age nor experience separated him from them. He had taken a disproportionate amount of abuse on his way up the hierarchy, but he had never viewed this as a justifiable excuse for exacting revenge on his own juniors, who, after all, had their own experiences to overcome. This generosity did, however, fall short of governing his behaviour in love. Here he had found new Lucille Rojos to hurt and be hurt by. He had despised those weak enough to be hurt by him and fought those enough like him to be able to hurt in kind. He had found every deviation of her he could, any girl with anything of the Lucille about her at all, and had become familiar with them all in the hope that in the end the one face he had looked for in all of them would be forgotten, and Lucille Rojo would cease to be the face of his story.

Earlier that day he had watched her at the barber's with Largo and Josip and had felt a curious lack of nostalgia. Now, as the car travelled towards the end of the Tibidabo road, he was able to tell why. Nostalgia could only be felt for what was recognised as dead, the property of a different time and a past self. Lucille Rojo was an on-going concern.

Chapter Two

8.15 p.m. – the Rojo hacienda

Knowing him for her whole life had not made her any abler a judge of her father's moods; they were his own business, too distant and self-referential for her to grasp. As a consequence Lucille Rojo had struggled to create a sane and sober picture of her father, who, though several inches shorter than herself, still appeared as a giant, capable of returning her into her childhood by the simple raising of an eyebrow. Unlike other girls Lucille did not seem to mind this state of frozen development, and, much to her mother's distaste, neither did her father, the Don.

Perhaps the clearest expression of this unnatural attachment was voiced over the breakfast table as daily each would recount to the other the dreams they had had the night before. To hear these exchanges would be to realise that the Don and his daughter were rarely out of one another's dreams.

'Is anything the matter, Pepe?'

The Don put his fork down and looked up at his daughter. The first dream had been terrible, the second also, and the last dream of the night the worst he had ever suffered. Moreover, the early evening nap that he had hoped would have a relaxing effect had done exactly the reverse. Instead of enjoying a few hours' sleep that could have put some distance between him and his anxieties he had instead played a ridiculous mind game centring, though it seemed impossible to credit it now, on whether the wind would blow over his bed or not.

'You look as though you're thinking of something. Is there anything the matter?'

The Don pushed his plate away and stared at his daughter in a way that he hoped would seem fatherly and, for a moment, thought of telling her the truth.

'No, nothing, nothing's the matter, I think I'm just drifting a little . . .'

'Drifting where?' Lucille said, sounding far more abrupt than she had meant to.

The Don hesitated and groaned inwardly. This was his trouble. He could not resist a challenge.

'I was only thinking of my first meeting with your mother. I don't think you've ever been told about that, have you?'

'Tell her, Braulio, I think I'd like to be reminded of this,' his wife urged him from over the table, animated, or so it seemed, by an uncharacteristic interest in what he had to say.

Don Rojo cleared his throat and turned towards her. His marriage, and the memory of their first meeting, was not a place they had ever ventured back to before. When the urge to talk about it had taken hold of him in the past a quick glance from her was enough to remind him that a precious memory ought never to be reduced to an anecdote.

'Well, what are you waiting for?' said his wife derisively, and cast a look at the Don that she hoped he would associate with disapproval.

The Don cleared his throat again, caught his wife's glance and wondered, for a moment, whether to pay any attention to it.

'Your grandparents led me to her,' he began, conscious that he was acting like a man being watched. 'I had pestered them for a diving-suit,' he continued, 'a type of deep-water outfit. This was a month or two before my sixteenth birthday. My mother had wanted to buy me a new one, but my father advised caution – in those days it was always a question of funds. In the end my father had his way and we answered an advert placed in the local paper by your mother's parents. Now, I was very excited, but when we arrived at their house your mother refused to leave her room and surrender the suit! Her father had to explain that he'd spoilt her and suggested that I might go upstairs and persuade her to part with it myself.'

The Don could feel his wife's presence over the table, and hoped that it was only an affectionate slap she wanted to give him. Smiling to himself, he began to expand the thread of the story.

'Remember, I had never met a stubborn girl before, so it threw me a little when she led me into her bathroom wearing the diving-suit I had come to collect . . .'

'And did I remove this suit, Braulio?' his wife interrupted.

'You did, but first you stood with it on under the shower to prove that it could keep the water out and later, when I touched your skin, I could feel that it was still dry and that the suit had done its job.'

Lucille grinned awkwardly. Her father had used a voice which, though his, she had never heard before. It was a voice from whose world she felt excluded, and it emphasised a growing apart that she, at least, had felt keenly for some time now.

'You can leave the table if you like,' her mother announced without warmth.

'Thank you . . . for dinner.' Lucille stood up and, purposefully avoiding eye contact with either of her parents, walked out of the dining room into the adjoining hall.

The Don grinned broadly, his wife less so.

'I didn't sleep well last night.'

'I know,' his wife replied.

'It was nightmares.'

His wife nodded, her manner neither offhand nor committed.

The Don smiled weakly in an attempt to imitate her mood but, unfortunately for him, feigned indifference was not something he could switch on and off. His wife, however, could, and this meant that no mood or attitude she adopted was, he felt, entirely trustworthy. He was canny enough to realise that this was not the fault of subterfuge on her part, but merely a deterrent she employed to police her fierce temper in the face of frequent provocation.

'I knew you were dreaming because you were thrashing about the bed making a bloody noise,' his wife said uninterestedly, 'but I don't expect to hear what any of it was about . . .'

'Because you wouldn't be interested if I told you,' the Don interjected.

'No, because I'm not Lucille and unlike her I've less time for dipping in and out of your indulgent bullshit.'

The Don's weak smile broke back into an open grin, one he was especially proud of since he was sure it was his wife's aim to goad him into an open-handed slap. He was aware that, despite her protestations to the contrary, she had developed the capacity to enter into his dreams and literally experience them, moment to moment, at the same time as himself. As such she knew that the first dream had been terrible because things that had not happened yet, and things which might never happen, happened. The second dream had been terrible too because of what had already occurred in the first, and the third dream, which was by far the worst, existed in a place that defied interpretation. The Don got up, and without a word, began the ascension to his observatory, where, his wife assumed, he would be able to work things through to his satisfaction.

8.30 p.m. – the upper Tibidabo crossroads

Clusters of armed men lay on both sides of the road.

All wore the same indifference, an indifference born from the fact that it would be as easy for them to kill as it would be for them not to. Few of them had noticed the car that had stopped in front of the roadblock. Their commander, a well-fed and cynical man, had marched them in circles for days so that now, despite the damp, many were grateful for the opportunity to rest. Many more had forgotten duty altogether and fallen asleep in groups of three and four to the strange rhythms of the drizzle. Even their commander, wiping the moisture off his glasses, had caught himself drifting off into a mild trance bought on by the half-light of dusk. The week had been marked by an ugly run-in with a group of refugees who, fearing the soldiers, had hidden themselves in the loft of a barn not far from the commander's estate. The meeting had not ended happily. The commanding officer had drawn his men into a tight ring, so that they were all in sight of one another, and called through the trapdoor for the occupants to give themselves up. His words were chosen carelessly.

He shook his head. The barn had gone up like a torch and the strong wind that was everywhere that night had probably carried the smell of burning bodies across the Tibidabo woods to his estate, where his daughter had settled down to do her homework. He could not help but visualise the exaggerated move her head made when she pretended to think, and her nose twitching as the unfamiliar smell of charred flesh had entered her room through the open window. He stared blankly into the road and at the car parked in front of his roadblock.

Josip recognised him immediately as Raul Alcazar, commander of the Tereul garrison, a man who included in his vast repertoire of boasts the ability to kill without hatred. They had not met since Josip's conscription four years earlier when, having identified him as a lanky but impudent streak of country piss, Alcazar had subjected him to the 'treatment'. Josip's quasi-religious stubbornness, hatred of authority and indifference to physical pain kept him going for two months, at which point Alcazar had ordered the treatment to be lifted. For the last three months of his training Josip had been left to do what he liked.

Thundering up the bank like a man desperate to right an earlier wrong, Alcazar growled in his most theatrical parade voice, 'Get out of the car, one at a time.'

The men did as he said and lined up on the road, Josip standing directly in front of the car's lights, his bright red hair turning a burning gold. Alcazar nodded his head in recognition and turned his attention to the Captain. By his uniform he was able to tell he was nominally on the same side as this man.

'I'm looking out for would-be vigilantes, real political animals . . . you know the type.'

The Captain looked at him impassively.

'That wouldn't be you, would it, Captain?'

Josip smirked and Largo and the Captain followed suit, with only Ali, usually the most juvenile of the four, retaining his composure. None of them felt in any real danger, however. There had been roadblocks put up every night to stop the recent spate of assassinations, but it was a tacit convention that no one in uniform would stop anyone else in the same dress.

'Hmmm . . . I don't know whether any of you look mean enough to be assassins, *because that's the sort of person I'm looking out for*,' said Alcazar with a bored emphasis.

'What do we look like, then?' Ali spluttered back concernedly.

'Like nice young men,' said Alcazar slowly.

Ali looked over at the Captain, whose smirk was transforming into a confrontational sneer.

Alcazar allowed himself to smile. It was a smile that belied the smugness of a man who believed he would never be anyone's victim.

'Now I hope you don't find me impertinent, I don't for a single minute believe that you or any of your men are implicated in any criminal activity,' Alcazar continued, addressing the Captain directly, 'but with things being as they are, we must take care . . .'

Alcazar stopped and smiled. The rain had started to fall in steady sheets and Alcazar could feel the water seeping through his coat and on to his shoulders.

'Why can't the rain use itself up and stop, eh?'

The Captain's face broke and he returned a smile. Despite himself he found Alcazar an appealing character.

Alcazar looked at the stripes on Josip's shoulder and winked.

'I've already held you up longer than I had to, but I wanted to get a good look at what your new friends looked like, Corporal.'

Josip, looking a little bewildered, nodded happily.

'Sergeant!'

'Sir!'

'I think we can move your mother's furniture off the road now and allow these gentlemen to get on with their business.'

Still smiling, Alcazar shook hands with all four men and returned to his perch by the side of the road. It had been a long time since he had seen Josip. Time, fortunately, had been a great healer. If it had been anything else then they would probably all have died at its hands by now, he reflected, and he settled on to his folding chair, hoisted his umbrella up and lit a cigarette. As a rule it was difficult for him to think of anyone for very long without becoming engrossed in himself, and in a few minutes he had forgotten about the car he had let through his roadblock.

The moon, by way of the skylight, divided the observatory into two halves – Don Rojo occupying the lit half, the music from his daughter's record-player filling the other half. The music, fast and unrhythmic, reminded him of a record he could only half remember from a period of his life he had largely forgotten. Averting his eyes from the wall nearest to him, he began to inspect the objects, both bought and acquired, that grew out of the floor of his room. There were a lot of them. Too many for someone who had sung the praises of a spartan life. Too many to be certain that this life had the consistency he thought it had, only days earlier.

Slowly he stretched his legs out from the stool he was sitting on and ran his hands over his stomach. This did nothing to ease the cramp in his legs and only highlighted the foolishness and discomfort of sitting in a half-lit room by himself. He knew he was there because it was time to face down certain problems, but unsurprisingly he found himself unwilling to begin this task. His usual way of facing problems was to not answer them and, after a period of time had passed, to pretend they were not relevant any more. Groaning loudly, and not altogether seriously, he got up and looked around his room for some appropriate distraction.

What he saw did not please him. Medals courtesy of men he hated rested on the shoulders of the busts of men he hated even more. Books he had never read, but arranged in colour schemes, collected dust. Books he wished he had never read rested by ones he had pretended to read (and broken the backs of), whilst below them on the floor lay stacks of unopened parcels, their contents and senders' intentions a matter of indifference to him now. If in one move he could have turned everything around, then destroyed everything else, he would have, but the moment the thought struck him had been spent entertaining it and not acting, so as the second passed so did the chance.

Downstairs the music had stopped playing and he

could hear his daughter talking loudly into the telephone. His resolve to get used to the device had petered out so that now, each time it rang, his hair would still stand on end. A wide range of pseudo-psychological explanations was dredged up to appease his family, and their amusement at his reluctance either to answer, or to talk to, the phone, and by and large they succeeded. It did not take him very long, however, to abandon them, since the Don could see through his explanations and knew them for what they were, a lot of old crap employed to cover his basic fear of people, people he could not see. The telephone, and the invisible people at the other end of it, encapsulated this fear. It comforted him to think that if he had chosen a career other than politics, or politics in a less violent climate, this fear would be annulled, would not even be his to annul. But comforting as this thought was, it was not true. And Don Rojo had a commitment to truth.

Crossing the room, he opened the door leading to the staircase, not to the extent that anyone would see it was open, but enough for him to overhear the conversation his daughter was having with Antonio, her Juan of the moment.

He listened for a minute or two and snorted angrily. Lucille's style was impressive. She seemed adept at manoeuvring around the promises and clichés he had once proudly held up as the true proofs of love. Far from upsetting him, her professionalism allowed the Don to draw parallels between his age and hers. It was a feeling he was so used to that his treatment of it was almost mechanical. Its upshot told him that whatever else he was, he, Don Rojo, was a survivor. *The* survivor. He stiffened his lips and straightened his back at the thought.

His attention now returned to the conversation downstairs. Lucille's speech was flat and inattentive. To follow it would be to doubt whether she was in love at all, which pleased the Don for a number of reasons, not least for the fact that Antonio, though cosmically insignificant, was still capable of inflaming the Don's more violent side. Antonio was smooth, wealthy, insubstantial, arrogant and curiously unpleasant. One did not want to give him any more thought than was necessary, and yet his strange mixture of evils gave him a place in the Don's imagination he scarcely deserved. And this seemed, to the Don at any rate, to be the whole point of Antonio.

Lucille put the phone down and made towards her room.

'Lucille.'

'Pepe.'

'Who was that you were talking to?'

'Antonio Mayle, Pepe.'

'What did he ring for?'

'To arrange a date. He wants to take me out later tonight.'

'And you're going to go?'

'Yes.'

'Why, because you really want to or because you think you have to?' the Don asked hopefully.

'I want to, or else I would have told him I didn't want to,' Lucille answered patiently.

'Then remember no boy, no matter how charming, has any luck unless you already want to do whatever he has in mind.'

Lucille smirked as though she had heard a dirty joke.

'I'll remember that, Pepe.'

For a moment the drizzle lapsed, faltered for a few seconds, and then broke into heavy rain. The Don noticed water on his shoulder. The skylight window was open.

The two men stood arguing outside the only phone box on the Tibidabo road, the richer of the two dressed in a felt coat, the other in the uniform of a civil guard. Of the two, the one in the uniform seemed the most conscious of the rain.

'I can't accept it, it's just not right for me to keep leaning on you like this.'

Antonio Mayle pushed the notes farther into his friend's palm.

'Simon, how long have I known you?'

'For ages, we've known each other for ages . . .'

'And have I ever once begrudged you money when you needed it?'

'You haven't but . . .'

'So take the money and stop making a meal of this shit.'

'Antonio, please, listen to what I have to say . . .'

'Simon' – Antonio laid an almost sisterly stress on the name – 'you're beginning to embarrass me.'

'That's the last thing I want to do, but if you'll just let me explain . . .'

'It doesn't interest me. If you don't have money and I do, then you're welcome to mine. In my position you'd do the same for me, so stop making me feel so generous.'

Simon took the money. There would never be a day when he had money and Antonio didn't but that was never going to be the point. Simon, like most other people he knew, hated Antonio.

'You take care now, okay, don't go around acting like a big girl, I know what you're like.'

Simon nodded mutely and watched Antonio skip over a puddle to his car, which was parked halfway up the bank. Guiding Antonio on to the Tibidabo road, Simon forced a smile which Antonio failed to notice. It was clear from the way his head was turned that he was already set upon his next destination. Simon waited until the car had driven off into the distance before he began to walk home.

He used to think that Antonio was all right. A bit of a rogue but, basically, all right. This was before his wife had told him she had enjoyed sex with Antonio on at least two occasions and, given the choice, would do so again. Simon had resolved to tell Antonio what a bastard he thought he was. He had got as far as starting to but, sensing his own unease, had stopped himself and made a joke of the whole thing. Revenge, in any case, was a dish best served cold, and Simon put off the confrontation until he could savour the effects. But time had the opposite effect and it was soon clear that Simon was more afraid of his friend than his wife. In the end he had done nothing.

It took Simon a minute or two to realise he was in tears.

Antonio checked his watch and changed gear. Outside, the clouds were moving like a team of ships dragging everything beneath them into the sea. The air in the car certainly felt comparable to that of a submarine, humid and clammy with only the faint aroma of perfume to offset the thick stench of rusting tin. Antonio, however, was indifferent both to the rain and to the deteriorating condition of his father's car. It was surprising, he thought, how good it felt to help out a friend. It was like he told Simon, without your friends you're nothing. In fairness, though, Simon had been becoming less and less of a friend; somewhere down the line he had lost his edge, his confidence had gone, and now he didn't know where to look for it. Antonio lit a cigarette. Life was hard on weak men. Without a strong will everything worked the wrong way for you. He changed back into second gear. Such moral thinking was affecting his driving. There were better things to do than waste time thinking about friends who thought of nothing except getting pissed, borrowing money off you and then doing something stupid with it. It seemed inconceivable to Antonio that any of these friends spent as much time worrying about him. For what it was worth his friends, selfish as they were, were all he had, but it was *because of them* that they were all he had. At least he knew, unlike them, that no situation stayed the same for very long, that the game kept moving on.

Stopping at Raul Alcazar's roadblock, he announced who he was and where he was going with a sneer characteristic of the vanity that nurtured it.

Raul Alcazar wanted to punch this kid in the mouth, punch him in the mouth many times, but form dictated that he let him through. Not all things, however, were dictated by form, and in Alcazar's opinion the boy's chances of lasting the night's distance were no better than fair to middling. Worse, he hoped.

Chapter Three

---

9 p.m. – the Tibidabo road

Now that the banks of the River Ebro had broken, the earth and sky had become indistinguishable, with water pouring forth from both. 'It's so black out there,' whispered Ali, his words trembling in naive awe.

'Ali?'

'What?' blurted Ali, with the surprise of a child woken from a trance.

'If you've something to say about the sky do it the kindness of looking in its general direction.'

Ali felt his shoulders tingle as he realised that for the past five minutes he had been staring at the Captain lovingly.

'If you keep looking at me like that people are going to start to talk,' the Captain muttered clumsily, upset that he had brought attention to this private, but innocent, thing.

This was not the first time that Ali had been caught looking at the Captain. He had been watching the Captain for some years now and consequently decided to be as much like him as he could, whilst remaining as true to himself as this ambition would allow. Everything about the Captain excited and interested him. Ali was

31

like a girl who had a favourite type of boy. The Captain was his type; Josip being too rural, Largo too ugly and his own type too disposed towards hectic self-doubt. It was his hope that in hindsight people would view the Captain and himself as a pair, that they would be spoken of in the same breath and remembered with the same warmth. Everything he had done, since leaving school and joining the army, had been performed with this aim in mind.

The Captain, four years above Ali at school, was like no one he had ever met before. In this the Captain was the rule and not the exception, as Ali already knew a number of unique people, but where the Captain differed from the others was in Ali's ability to identify with him. Firstly, and most obviously, the Captain had personified an attitude that Ali wished one day to carry off as his own. The fearlessness of the Captain's aggression, and his contempt for its consequences, touched Ali in a way that exceeded mere admiration. More important for Ali was the realisation that the Captain's combative arrogance sat beside other hidden qualities that he admired equally, if not more, than the louder ones. And yet the Captain never made an effort to draw attention to these subtler features, preferring to act as though he had not even noticed them. The reason for this, Ali decided, was that the Captain was a complicated person who pretended, for the sake of safety, to be a simple one. In this the Captain was partially successful since, peering behind his qualities, Ali recognised their fundamental unity, how each quality shared the same mother and father. Leadership and a way with women. Simple but elusive skills that the Captain had decided to hide himself behind. Skills that Ali was quick to attach a religious significance to, believing that if he were to grasp them, every other problem in his life would take care of itself. If he was able, under the Captain's instruction, to pick up leadership, then he would stand a chance with a girl, but to fail in one would be to fail in the other, and failure in either of these meant failure in everything else. The situation, from whatever angle he approached it, was a bind, but as Ali had never attempted to *do* anything before, and therefore never experienced real failure, the risks seemed worth the prize.

What Ali chose to see as the Captain's way with women meant, in practice, a way with specific women. It was probably his appreciation of *these* women that made Ali realise what he would forfeit if he were to give up his attempts at self-improvement. What puzzled him, though, was the way these girls seemed to do nothing for the Captain. How the Captain could let girls like Fialla, Muerta and Aria slip through his hands, without withdrawing to his quarters in grief for a month, astonished Ali. These women were striking and distinctive, moving proof of beauty's indifferent hierarchy. Ali had been particularly fond of Aria, a tall Basque with large green eyes and knee-high riding boots that appeared to be made of ivory. It was true that she, like the others, held him in open contempt and, for that matter, now held the Captain in open contempt too, but this did not make the Captain's attitude any less baffling. Despite expressing his regret that these girls now hated him, the Captain, on the whole, seemed blissfully unaware of the value of what had once been his to handle and lose. It was not until Josip pointed out Lucille Rojo, a tall girl with a large mouth and beige skin, that Ali began to understand the Captain's reticence towards all the others.

The moment Lucille introduced herself to Ali was perfect. Lucille, celebrating the Captain's twentieth birthday and uncharacteristically drunk, had turned a large basket over, taking its lid off and wearing it on her head as though it were a hat. Then, removing a sabre from the wall, and carefully balancing herself on one leg, placed its point under the neck of a large dog. The Captain had reprimanded her in some way or other but, ignoring him, she had turned to Ali, dropped her bottom lip and winked. It was the sexiest thing he had seen in his life, and from there on in he was prepared to fall in love with her whenever she willed it.

For the following few weeks Ali had had it bad; days passed but God failed to lead him out of temptation – there was just Lucille, morning and evening. Josip had tried to joke Ali out of his pain by telling him that Lucille worked on a first come, first served basis and, to put it frankly, Ali had arrived too late. A year passed. Lucille broke up with the Captain and took up with Antonio. If only Ali had known that he would have spent a whole year thinking about that single evening he would have said something on the night, the ambiguity and several possible interpretations of the moment having long ceased to interest him. But his feelings continued with a fierce and unforgiving regularity. He just wanted her and that was an end to it. Josip advised him to dwell on his lust; by concentrating on the carnal he would cease to love her, which would leave him free to act on her. This may have worked for Josip but it did not work for Ali. Again and again he would appeal to the higher emotions to fudge the practical – Lucille was a little too perfect to be desirable, too well rounded for him, not impulsive enough, a daddy's girl, and so forth. But the deceptions were puerile; he still wanted her and it was impossible for him to believe that one day he would not have her.

Eventually he approached the Captain with his problem, secure in the knowledge that the Captain had once been in the same situation himself. Ali had spoken with the seriousness of a teenager enjoying his first forays into manhood; brave in the presentation of his vulnerability but blind to his own self-absorption. His argument was simple; since nothing in life was as large as his pain, there was nothing else in his life he could take seriously, all other things seeming ridiculous or trivial in comparison. Surely something as painful as this, he implored, must amount to more than just another adolescent's broken heart?

The Captain was neither angry nor amused at this question and encouraged Ali to go on, listening patiently to his talk of disturbed sleep and recurring dreams, without once interrupting to say that his own pain had been greater or more intense. The two had carried on talking for hours like old friends and, after several drinks, the Captain had finished for the evening by telling Ali that he should risk being himself more and worry less. Things would work out in the end.

Never in the history of conversation, Ali thought, had such banality felt so reassuring or so true. The two had become the firmest of friends and, a month later when the Captain visited him with the offer of work, Ali seized his chance with both hands. As a consequence of this decision he would know, within three hours, whether he loved the Captain enough to kill Lucille's father, Don Rojo.

Ali turned around and peered at the Captain again; he looked asleep but his face still spoke to Ali, it said that everything was going to be all right. Ali shut his eyes and tried to hold on to this thought for as long as he could.

'Are you awake?' Ali opened his eyes but realised at once that Josip was talking to the Captain.

Josip nudged the Captain off his shoulder. The Captain yawned loudly, rubbed his face and peered out of the car window. For some reason he had expected it to be morning. With every sign post on the Tibidabo road taken down because of the war, it was difficult to tell exactly how far they had come. In the distance he could see the vague outline of a huge stage and large clusters of people gathering around it. Neither helped explain where they were since, on any normal night, neither would have been there.

The rain was less heavy than before but still powerful enough for the Captain to hear it landing on the waters of the River Ebro, which had now risen to flank both sides of the road. 'We must be close to the phone booth,' he whispered, and then repeated himself so that the others could tell that he was asking a question and not stating a fact.

'Nearly there. In fact, Largo, stop the car here, I need a piss before I make the phone call,' said Josip.

Swerving carelessly, Largo turned the car into the bank, knocking its fortifications and the sandbags that served as a flood barrier into the dark waters of the Ebro. 'Pull back or he'll fall straight into the river,' laughed Ali. 'Never mind the river,' Josip cursed, 'the fucking door won't open.'

Largo grimaced. The car, stolen from the used parts depot, had been one of the first of its kind, and was now barely roadworthy. 'Treat it gently, there's no use tugging at it like a madman,' Largo said authoritatively. 'Nothing works if you pull and tug at it.'

'Here, let me have a go,' offered Ali, bending his arm back into Josip's face and shifting his torso into the back seat. 'What you need to do is shove back and then pull up.' The Captain watched Josip's ears shake, a familiar sign that he was about to lose his temper. 'Get out of it, for Christ's sake,' yelled Josip, pushing Ali forward into the front of the car. Then, throwing himself on to his back, so that his shoulders were on the

Captain's lap, Josip swung his legs round and kicked the door off its hinges. A cold wave of rain flew into the car, as if it were the deck of a ship, making each of its occupants shiver and recoil. Josip, for his part, was already out in the storm, his puttees knee deep in muck, as he scrambled down the mudslide to the only phone box on the Tibidabo road. The river was close enough to lap at the wooden base of the booth and, Josip guessed, it would be minutes and not hours before it toppled into the black water. Given the circumstances his piss could wait until he had made the phone call. Taking an old ticket out of his pocket and unfolding it, he dialled the number of the Rojo hacienda.

A voice answered at the other end.

Josip mouthed a few words, waited for a reply, received none and replaced the receiver. Then, scrambling up the bank as fast as he could, he stumbled up to the car and took a piss over the road.

Largo, wrapped like a small animal in an army-issue grey coat, sat on the car bonnet scraping mud off it, his legs not quite reaching the ground. Growling loudly, he rolled off the car and pointed to Ali. 'Look at him, he's fallen asleep again.'

Josip whistled with disbelief and pulled open Ali's door. Sure enough Ali, who only minutes earlier was offering him advice on how to dislodge a jammed door, was fast asleep, his narrow, mink-like head buried in his jacket.

Josip stopped himself from wiping mud into the sleeping boy's face for fear of hypocrisy. Falling asleep, whenever the opportunity presented itself, was a skill he shared and, at his estimate, was probably the only skill Ali possessed that hadn't required hard work. For all that, Ali did not look particularly at peace with himself, his eyelids flickering up and down like moths' wings. 'Look at that, he's dreaming, the little bugger's so *fast* asleep he's dreaming,' squealed Largo, who, if it had not been for this diversion, would have been complaining about the smashed door. 'How can you bank on someone like that?' Largo continued triumphantly. 'Thank God he's not on sentry duty, that's all I can say.' With his head back in the car, Josip lit a cigarette and, ignoring Largo's righteous protestations concerning Ali's neglect of duty, blew a line of smoke into his sleeping friend's face. Smiling benevolently, he wondered what was causing Ali's sleeping face such disquiet.

Ali's dream was neither savoury nor coherent. *It began with Lucille's head being kissed so hard that every strand of her hair was covered in saliva. Next, using the end of a spade, Ali outlined the tips of her nipples, leaving traces of earth, from a freshly dug grave, over her blouse. Other things happened too, and by the end the physical had moved into the transcendent as he manoeuvred his way into her . . .*

'WAKE UP!'

Ali did not stir. There, under the car's headlights were three bodies, one man and two women. He recognised one of the women. Her yellow hair was caked in blood.

'What?'

'You've fallen asleep again,' Largo said brusquely.

Ali wiped his eyes. The last thing he could remember properly was the car stopping for Josip to take a piss. His head felt like it was at the wrong end of a drunken memory. 'How long was I asleep for?'

'No more than an hour, I'd say. You know, I'd watch it if I were you, you've probably got some kind of sleeping disease . . .'

'Where's the Captain?' Ali said, ignoring Largo's friendly warning.

'Taking a leak. If your face is anything to go by you should take one too.'

'What's happened to Josip?'

'I'm here.'

Ali rubbed his eyes again and then the rest of his face, before asking, 'Are we all right for time?'

Josip checked his watch, allowing his broad shoulders to drop in an arc. They were not all right for time, they were not all right by ten minutes.

It was true that corruption existed before the republic, she would be the first to agree with that, but the advent of the republic had been corruption's second wind, its monetary shot in the arm. And her husband, the Don, had become its leading proponent. For Helena Rojo, this was probably the single most important factor in the view she currently took of her husband. As she thought little of money, and even less of those who prized it, this blackening of her husband's nature offered incontrovertible proof that he had changed and become a stranger to her.

'I suppose you'd rather have anarchy or dictatorship than the rule of capital and law,' he would argue in his defence.

'It's not that, Braulio, you know it's not. It's got nothing to do with those sorts of abstractions . . .'

'Helena, what do you have against us doing well? What's a perfectionist like you doing here, living so close to real people, having to suffer such close approximation to their grubby movements? Move to the clouds, they'd offer you greater happiness than anything I've conjured up . . . go on, go!'

The Don's argumentative style was fast, disingenuous and snappy, honed to perfection through years of hard political training. It had the undoubted merit of settling any argument, at the level of words, in his favour, but was of less use when dealing with issues he actually cared about.

His dishonest ease was, in actuality, an affectation, since the Don was never so comfortable with corruption as to not suffer from it greatly. The cause of his suffering was, for once, refreshingly obvious; like his wife he held a low opinion of corrupt people and found it distressing to think that honest men and women might view him as such a person. Unlike some, who accepted corruption as a mark of influence and standing, the Don, like a man susceptible to guilt after the act is done, suffered corruption as a burden of high office. His initial indifference towards it, coupled with his subsequent failure to identify himself as someone who benefited from it, earned him many enemies. After the first few months, however, it became easier to allow corruption to have its own way and learn. That whatever it would be like in an ideal world, corruption had much to recommend it.

Its practical administration was not as easy as he hoped it would be. Institutionalised dishonesty, like any system, brought with it its own paperwork, which, unlike the rest of office business, could not be hived off to an under-secretary or passed on to some other department. As a consequence the Don would find himself holed up for hours on end mulling over who could pay more for curfew exemption, Eutemio Pons, owner of the neighbouring hacienda, or Cosme Mujal, Lucille's clarinet teacher. He took no pleasure in these decisions as they drove home how little that side of himself had in common with the rest of his character. The Don's corruption could therefore mock his own view of himself as a man of substance and cast its untrustworthiness over every other area of his life it had so far left untouched. If it had not already brought him as low as those other 'politicians' he persisted in looking down upon, it *had* robbed him of the substance he considered necessary for his self-respect. The immediate effect of this occurred faster than he feared, as his wife and daughters seemed to afford him less and less consideration with each passing day. This was, he knew, no more than he deserved.

He had made the mistake of using those parts of

himself that were not corrupt to understand those parts that were, and driven himself mad at the hands of his own inconsistency. Without intending to, he now occupied a position in which it was impossible for him to tell the truth, either to his fellow politicians or even to close friends, so implicated was everyone in everyone else's business. Unwisely he had turned to his wife, desperate in the need to indulge in absolute truth and firm in the belief that through just *being truthful* about himself Helena would see him again for who he truly was, and understand everything. It had not worked out. It had been a mistake to have such faith in the mending power of honesty and a mistake to believe that the course of a life could change just because he wanted it to. His life was not something he could operate on, as though he had nothing to do with it, and it was far too late to make a clean break. Therefore he had resolved to make the best of the flawed person he had become and, in the course of this half-hearted compromise, he had helped drive both himself and his wife mad.

Whether Helena had always been a little mad, or whether he had actually driven her that way, was a question the Don often asked himself. She had certainly always had a terrible temper, but then, if he was to be honest, so had he. If the matter were to be put before a court of enquiry then, the Don feared, Helena would probably emerge with rather more credit than he would. At least her madness was a product of her angers and passions whilst his was the result of something rather less straightforward. More tellingly, while several people would testify to the Don having a slightly crazy streak in him, few would say the same thing of Helena. For most she was the composed head of a wilfully difficult family, a little intimidating maybe, but certainly not mad. Only the Don saw otherwise; he could see it on their first meeting and it was still there now. Perhaps this was because he was the only person who could draw madness out of her. Certainly the converse was true, as he had never met anyone else who could make his blood rise so quickly. Because of this he felt that the pressure was on her to control the effect she had on him, as the consequences of her failing to were often terrible. The trouble was that she felt exactly the same way about *him*, so that in effect the two assumed a bizarre responsibility for each other's anger.

Over time their arguments had grown less passionate, and more theoretical, as Helena Rojo's desperate overtures to her husband's conscience were replaced by more successful broadsides against his intellect.

'You equate freedom with safety and safety with your purse. Really, Braulio, when I think of you, and how you've changed, I think of a mouse gathering cheese rinds at the expense of a proper meal.'

'There's no point responding to you in your own terms, Helena, because I know you don't believe a word of what you're saying. Everything you say is just designed to hurt me and that's all. Besides, you're not blind, you can see how much we've gained.'

'Gained! How dare you allow your criminality to take credit for my hard work!'

Every so often the arguing would stop, the Don would make some conciliatory gesture, a small donation to a local charity or a private members' bill calling for land reform, and the house would return to an uneasy silence. Mutual antipathy would, however briefly, be buried, and Helena would become an exaggerated model of compliance in all things superficial. To her it seemed that during these periods the Don was forever trying to goad her into an open rage so that she could be blamed for the resumption of hostilities. She would shield herself from his provocations and try to ignore her feelings and not take the bait. The Don, of course, believed that she was doing precisely the same thing to him, and baited her merely as a way of protecting himself against her cold contempt. In the end it was usually Helena who would break first, since, of the two, it was Helena who found it harder to treat an abnormal situation normally. Delude herself as she might, years of living at war with her partner had ruined her self-possession. Just as she thought she was winning and beginning to act like a woman and not a girl, her temper would be upon her and years of wisdom would be lost in a fit of anger. It was a pattern set during their first summer together, twenty-five years earlier, and the start of an incredible battle that neither of them had yet won outright. The silence of the past two weeks had been the longest amnesty yet, but the tension in the house was becoming unbearable. And unlike their arguments in the past, *which had never really been about anything*, the fights of the past three years did not stop once the Don had enjoyed the last word. An unfortunate development that he was fully aware of.

'Braulio, I've made some coffee,' called Helena.

There was no answer from the observatory, and she noticed that her hands were shaking slightly.

For the past few weeks the Don had been in and out of the house at all hours, maintaining unusually high levels of secrecy for one so disposed towards talk. She knew that if she were to ask him what he had been doing, it would mean an argument, so she had held her peace. Nevertheless she found that her nervous tension, far from being buried, was channelled into the after-dinner ritual of preparing coffee for the Don. She usually had to call him twice before he came down.

'It's been ready for twenty minutes . . . twenty minutes.'

There was still no answer from the observatory. She could feel the anger filling up in her throat and knew that it would be there in her voice if she called again.

'Don't you realise that I've made this for *you*!' she hollered, conscious that as the pitch of her voice rose, it lost the authority it normally enjoyed. She first noticed this when, as a young bride still living with her in-laws, she and the Don would argue in hushed whispers so as to not wake his parents. On those occasions she sounded every inch his match but, at those points where she could no longer control her temper and her voice rose, the whole force of her argument began to sound like that of a little girl. She had actually brought this up with the Don, but all he claimed to remember was that most of their arguments were conducted in the nude and that Helena's large breasts would shake whenever her voice rose.

There was still no answer from the observatory. There was no answer, she decided, because the man she loved more than anyone else was treating her as less than a human being.

'I've made your coffee, IT'S MADE AND IT'S GET-TING COLD! Answer me . . .'

Helena, not sure whether she was shouting for effect or crying because she couldn't help it, doubled back into the kitchen and broke the coffee tray over the worktop. The sink filled with hot water, milk and sugar. For a minute she stood there, waiting for painless emissions of blood to come pouring from her hands. None came.

The door opened behind her and the Don strode in. He inspected the mess. Looking straight at her, he said, 'If you're still angry enough to want to break something else I can return later.' It would not be beyond her as once, returning home after an argument, he had found her methodically taking a hammer to a set of vases they had been given as a wedding gift.

'Why don't *you* break something,' she spat, defiantly, all thoughts of self-control forgotten now.

Believing that a loss of temper was expected of him at this point, the Don blustered unconvincingly, 'Clear

this up and learn to handle your tantrums . . . in whatever order you please. Grasp that and I may still be here
to listen to whatever your latest set of complaints is.'

Helena looked at the Don like she was daring him
to kill her.

The Don looked puzzled, genuinely surprised that
his patrician manner was having no effect. But this,
of course, was no reason to abandon it. 'I'm tired of
you, Helena, and tired of this. Just think of how long
it's been going on for.'

There was a muffled response which the Don failed
to catch. He strode out of the kitchen in the same
manner which he had entered it. It had been a long
time since he had been able to take his wife's pain
as seriously as his own, and this last performance
offered nothing for him to change his mind. To dignify
such a scene with seriousness would be to elevate
game-playing to an acceptable domestic sport. The
Don snorted like an aggravated dog. He was going
to have none of it.

It wasn't until he got to the steps that he hesitated.
For the last few minutes he had been led by habit,
and now that it had worn off, it left a current of
overwhelming foolishness in its wake. It seemed to
tell him that he had no right to be taken seriously
by his wife, *that he could not even argue with her
properly any more*. More importantly his wife's line of
attack puzzled him; it wasn't like her to be so openly
emotional or raw. He looked back at the kitchen door
and took a step towards it.

Helena stopped crying and sat up straight. Like the Don she too felt slightly foolish. Her last outburst was uncharacteristic, typical of her twenty years ago but not at all like her now. As with her very first confrontations with the Don, it had arisen out of nothing and vanished quickly. There was another thing too, something she had to tell the Don, something that had nothing to do with their arguments. It was to do with the strange phone call. Whatever it was had been eclipsed by hurt. The hurt it took to acknowledge that each encounter with her husband steadily degraded whatever feeling they still held for each other. It hurt because there was still plenty of care left and, even though they were unlikely to produce more, what remained was still strong enough to endure more pain. And this, in turn, meant the death of their love would not be a rushed or sudden affair.

The door opened for a second time and the Don walked in again. His wife looked different to him now, like a fifty-year-old woman who still considered him worth losing her temper over. He moved over to her and helped her up from her chair, slowly resting his hand on the nape of her neck. He spoke to her gently. She looked up and they embraced.

'Now tell me what's wrong.'

Helena closed her eyes. She had answered the phone and heard the warning. But to raise this subject would be to confront a problem that she was not versed in, a type of problem that had the power to scare her.

'Helena, tell me, what is it?'

Helena Rojo moved her head level with the Don's. So this was how it would end. She put her finger over her husband's lips and pressed her body against his.

'I want you to take me to bed, Braulio.'

Chapter Four

9.30 p.m. – the Perez-Barabo fair

The platform the Captain had spied earlier had been put there by the Perez-Barabo collective. The stage, and the various smaller tents and stalls that surrounded it, were all part of the St Bartholomew's Day fair organised by the syndicalist collective to appease its religious-minded constituency. Despite the heavy weather, large crowds of people had gathered in the rain-sodden fields, and the brief cessation in the downpour had been greeted with the lighting of a ceremonial bonfire.

The four men moved through the fair, leaving their car parked behind the small open-air restaurant. The Captain had decided that it was better to be behind schedule by a complete hour than by ten minutes, and since the other men were hungry and keen to stretch their legs no one had bothered to question this logic. Even though much of the fair had been reduced to marshland, the more enterprising parts of it were still standing, encouraging Largo and Ali to ask passers-by which of these remaining stalls was selling drink. The Captain and Josip lagged slightly behind them.

'Do you think the Don will have acted on our warning?' the Captain asked quietly.

'Maybe,' Josip replied, before adding under his breath, 'But I didn't actually speak to him.'

'*What!*' the Captain cried with surprise. 'Well, who did you speak to, then? One of the daughters? A maid who happened to be in the area at the time?'

'I think it was the wife.'

'And you found her responsive, I suppose?'

'To be honest, no. I think she thought I'd got the wrong number.'

'Well, what did she say?'

'Nothing . . . really.'

'So as far as we know the Don won't have got the warning.'

Josip smiled patiently. He was a year older than the Captain and, unlike his younger friend, spoke in the slow and gentle rhythms of the Aragon countryside. The difference was always apparent when heard next to the Captain's faster Catalan growl.

'I could call again if you like.'

'No, that would be pointless.'

'Why?'

The Captain paused for a moment. 'You know, even if you'd spoken to him he may have considered it a hoax . . .' The Captain allowed his voice to trail off. He knew that Josip had guessed that if he could get out of killing Don Rojo, he would. And yet it would not do to make this too obvious.

'You've got stronger reasons to want to kill him than any of the rest of us,' Josip said with half an eye on the Captain's reaction. 'If he hasn't got the warning all the better for you. And anyway, even if he did, you just said that he wouldn't act on it.' Josip smiled wryly at the way the Captain's face was stiffening, confirming his suspicion that his friend had accepted this task on the basis of a great anger and not cold calculation.

'That depends,' the Captain said hesitantly. 'He thinks too much of himself to believe anyone would kill him, but he *is* cautious and very paranoid . . .'

Josip nodded his head in agreement. 'I think you're right. He may sense the worst but he's too vain and proud a man to act on it. When we show, he'll be there.'

The Captain, unconsciously aping Josip, nodded purposefully. Having never mastered the silent language of intuition, he was inclined to turn to Josip in much the same way as the Greeks had consulted the Oracle at Delphi. Like the Greeks he trusted the guesswork of the Oracle over his own. But tonight he wished he was hearing different things.

'Since we've left things for an hour I doubt the girls will be there when we arrive,' the Captain said, hoping he wouldn't be contradicted.

'I don't know. Will they?' Josip was not unaware of the Captain's special interest in this area.

'I didn't realise I was asking a question.'

'Lucille ought to be out,' Josip continued, ignoring the Captain's discomfort. 'Lucille's out most of the time these days but Rosa should be at home. Still, if we're quick, I don't think she'll notice our coming and going . . .'

'You really think she will be?' the Captain interrupted.

'I don't want to sound heartless but didn't you think of any of these things earlier? And anyway, out of the two of us you should know more about her comings and goings than me.'

'I'm not asking you that type of question,' the Captain said defensively. 'In fact I'm not asking you anything at all. It's just that the more people there are in the house . . .'

'. . . the more of a problem there'll be for us,' Josip said, finishing his part for him.

'Yes,' the Captain intoned defensively, 'that's right.'

Josip looked down at his feet and sighed slightly. Like Largo, but unlike Ali and the Captain, Josip had enjoyed no formal education and was grateful for it. The educated, it seemed to him, were always quick to confuse help with offence. The best way around this, at least when dealing with the Captain, Josip decided, was to put oneself in a position of relative weakness by admitting to vulnerability. Then, and only then, would the Captain do likewise, allowing conversation to progress beyond guarded soliloquies.

'I don't know how I'd react if the Don's loving daughters decided to throw themselves in our path to save their daddy. Not that I'd think he'd let them, though,' Josip added quickly.

Much to his surprise the Captain grinned. 'Well, what do you think we bought the muscle along for?'

The Captain thumbed towards Ali, who was deep in argument with Largo. Despite the uniform he wore, the idea of Ali in *any* type of fight struck both men as slightly ridiculous. His presence amongst them that night could be explained by the desire to include a friend, rather than through operational necessity. The same was true of Largo. In the last instance only Josip and the Captain could be counted on to fight and they both knew it.

'Ali, as our first line of defence, eh? Word of his arrival should clear the house of any ladies, I grant you that.' Despite Ali's height and Persian appearance, which made him popular with middle-aged women, Josip was aware that girls of his own age found him an intense and troubling proposition.

The Captain nodded mindlessly, as if to keep the subject matter of the conversation at bay. 'You're right,' he said, 'but I think we may have left it a little late to warn the ladies of our arrival.'

The Captain only half believed this. A strange part of him *wanted* the girls to be there, the same part of him that ached to confront Lucille with his enduring love for her, but also the same side that would have to confront her father, the Don. If there was any inconsistency to this wish, he was as blind to it as he was to his other faults.

Josip, sensing what he took to be a lapse in the Captain's defences, yawned theatrically and said, 'It's unlike you to be pushed into something you don't want to do, especially when it's you putting peer pressure on yourself to do it.'

'Is that what you think I'm doing?'

'I don't know. Are you?'

The Captain started, as if to say something, but, finding he did not know what to say, let it go.

'I'm not going to repeat this,' Josip continued, 'but I wish we were doing something else tonight, and I know, in your heart, you do too.'

'Listen to me, Josip,' the Captain retorted, without any real conviction, 'whether we like it or not we've all volunteered for something there's no going back on, and I don't understand what you're trying to prove by forcing me to spell it out to you.' The Captain paused, for what he hoped would be taken for effect, and stared at Josip gravely. The only thing he could feel, within this affected overreaction, was weakness and, sensing this, Josip answered, 'I didn't mean to strip the lining off your bowels, it's just that I'm feeling a little shat up, that's all.'

The Captain clasped his hands behind his head and returned quickly to the part of the conversation they were both most comfortable with. 'Well, as long as he's the only one in the house we aren't going to mix him up with anyone else.'

'I know,' added Josip unnecessarily, 'though it isn't as though I'd recognise any of the Rojo women in the dark anyway.'

The Captain scowled, reminded again of his failure to mentally prepare for what was about to be done. One needed sleep before agreeing to do something like this. The bender at the barber's the night before hadn't exactly been the best preparation.

'All I mean is that you'd recognise them, wouldn't you?'

The Captain could not argue with that. There would be no trouble in recognising Helena Rojo, Lucille's mother. He had first met her in the family kitchen, lit by the cold sun of an October afternoon. Her large eyes had wandered up and down his body approvingly as she had stood to greet him. She had shaken his hand with a slow and sensual assertiveness and apologised for her appearance and for the laundry lying on the floor. Her ironical sighing and eye-rolling, twinned with her boyish cropped hair, accentuated her handsomeness, and from that day on she had become a pivotal feature in the Captain's fantasies. Though there had been little in the way of open flirtation, the Captain had enjoyed watching Helena garden in tight-fitting peasant clothes and unconsciously stored these scenes in his masturbatory imagination. Sensibly he had kept these thoughts from Lucille, partly because of their ridiculousness and partly because of their strength. Like Lucille, Helena carried a smile that drew one in but, like Rosa, her younger daughter, the smile exercised a cautionary distance. This meant that whilst the Captain felt Helena's approval of him he was left in no doubt that there was plenty she disapproved of as well. The fact that these conflicting attitudes sat so close together both flattered and unsettled him, as he slowly got to grips with the larger problem of the Don's outright hostility.

His ability to recognise Rosa would be less precise. Try as he might the Captain could not recollect meeting her, even though there was no doubt they had, in fact, met several times. His casual arrogance notwithstanding, it was unusual for the Captain to bury the memory of meeting a girl, as he found nothing admirable in blanking people he already knew; which was the offence Rosa thought him guilty of. As he had only ever met Rosa in her sister's company it was unsurprising that, of the two girls, Lucille had left the more marked impression on him, a fact Rosa found difficult to accept. Whereas Lucille's appeal was disabling in its immediacy, Rosa's was more subtle, something the Captain was aware of but not drawn to. Their meetings felt like they had been invented to fill a missing link in social history, and not as experiences with realities of their own. Although other people had been quick to fill in the gaps, this help had not been motivated by a benevolent love of the facts. What upset the Captain most about this was not the gossip of others, but the one thing of Rosa's that *had* left its mark on him – her art, or rather a single painting.

The Don had hung the unfortunate object over his desk during his term in office, thus making it impossible for one not to have an opinion, partly informed by pity, about the painting. Muerta Astro, the Captain's girlfriend at the time, worked in the records office and walked past it every day. In her opinion the rot started with the Don himself. What did the hardest administrator in the building think he was doing to his reputation by hanging up crap like that? she had thundered. In her opinion it resembled an ugly child's drawing, looming over a place where business was conducted, a

place *where no one had the option to look the other way.*
His daughter might be a little backward, even in need of
gentle encouragement, but government buildings were
no place for a father's misplaced compassion.

The Captain had agreed that the painting was certainly a mistake, not a deliberate or mannered one, but
the inept result of love carried to an illogical extreme.
This charitable response was, the Captain felt, vin-
dicated by the Don's awkward handling of his own
gesture. The Don seemed to ignore its presence (did he
think that he had to take ultimate responsibility for its
creation?), and carry on as if it was not there, adding to
its general displacement and making it something that
no one, apart from voracious Muerta, felt comfortable
commenting on.

The painting depicted a large donkey drinking from
a puddle and what may or may not have been a small
calf attempting to do the same thing. Both animals had
been drawn badly and coloured in superimposed brown
crayon, giving them the appearance of chocolate toys.
Their distinguishing mark being eyes which were too
large for their respective heads.

Muerta, with typical staged cattiness, had suggested
that the painting alluded to nothing so much as an
engagement between enthusiasm and limited ability.
The Don, entering the room just as she had finished
speaking, had asked her to repeat herself. Thinking on
her feet, Muerta blurted out that the donkey's eyes
would look better if they were replaced by milk bottle
tops, and, incredibly, the Don had said that he would

take the painting home and put the idea to his daughter. The following day the painting returned with the golden foil of milk bottle tops spread lovingly across each of the donkey's eyes. The Don had thanked Muerta for her suggestion and given her the rest of the day off.

That night, after she and the Captain had made love, Muerta expressed remorse over her joke; the fact that it could be taken seriously emphasised the damage her tongue was capable of inflicting on the weak and trusting. She had asked the Captain questions about Rosa. Had he met her? Was it true that she was mad? Did she really cry as much as people said she did and, if so, why did she? The Captain replied that he knew nothing about her beyond the painting, that he had broken with Lucille months ago, and in any case, that whole period of his life felt like it had happened to someone else. He was with Muerta now, she was the only thing that interested him and they should talk about something else.

But before they fell asleep Muerta had said something else. She had told him that she would watch the Don, working alone in that room, and look at the lids of his eyes, and then at the donkey in the painting, and feel sorry for them both without ever really knowing why.

This was not what the Captain wanted to be thinking of now.

'Did you ever get to the bottom of why Rosa went mad and ran up to her room that time you forgot to say goodbye to her?' Josip said to break the silence.

'No, I didn't,' answered the Captain.

'Hmmm, I don't know too much about her myself,

just that she's got one of those faces you forget in between meetings . . .'

If Josip had hoped that the Captain was ready to pick up a conversational lead, he was disappointed. His friend's expression suggested that the overproduction of interest concerning the Rojos should, temporarily at least, be halted. This was not such a loss since something else was now catching Josip's attention.

Ahead of them, on a hastily erected platform, balanced on a pile of sandbags, stood a row of girls, the oldest of which was still a little short of full adulthood. All of the girls were of a dark-haired, dark-eyed, country complexion, and each, in her own way, reminded Josip of how the girls that had figured in his own past may have appeared, in the years preceding his acquaintance with them.

He nudged the Captain. 'That one over there'll be Aria in a few years.' The girl in question had legs unusually long for the slight body that they held up and eyes out of all proportion, in beauty, to her face.

'What about her over there?' piped Largo greedily.

'She's under ten, you sick bastard.'

'She's my height, though.'

Josip looked over at Largo wearily. The idea of him using his height as a prop in the seduction of a pubescent, though too ridiculous to entertain seriously, was still not impossible.

'Take thirty and sort us out for drinks,' said Josip, stuffing a pile of Republican army banknotes into Largo's hand.

Largo, aware that he was somehow being undercut, turned and limped towards the tent selling wine and beers, upset at the pain involved in watching the unattainable perform at such close range. He still had some way to go before getting over the events of that morning and he sensed he was unlikely to do this without a chance to sleep things off. If time, or the Captain, had afforded him sleep, he would be able to feel more confident about going on. As things were he was close to over-coding, his internal voices getting faster and vaguer by the minute. Sleep. A few hours' sleep and normality would be free to reassert itself.

Trudging over to the beer tent, and the few muddied benches that were acting as a makeshift bar, Largo could feel each step becoming more of an effort than the last. Though the rain had stopped, the patch of ground he was passing over had turned into sticky yellow clay, most of which was collecting along the ends of his trousers. By the time he had got to the tent he was feeling several pounds heavier, his trousers clinging like damp sacks to his legs.

'I'll have eight bottles of beer and a bag of nuts please,' he ordered as loudly as he could, his head not quite level with the plank that was serving as the bar.

The girl behind the bar stared down at him festively, looking, or so he hoped, as though she had enjoyed a few beers herself. Gently rubbing her breasts above his face, she pointed over to where the Captain was standing with Josip and asked, 'Who's your boyfriend?'

Not sure whether to ignore her or not, Largo repeated

his request, in a tone that he was sure was more authoritative. 'I'll have eight bottles of beer. And a bag of nuts.'

'Eight whole bottles of beer, why, it's a wonder you keep so thin, you . . .'

'They're not all for me,' Largo cut in. 'I have friends, you know,' and he gesticulated happily, but seriously, in the Captain's direction.

The girl's eyes followed the direction of his arm and, holding a beer bottle to her heart, she exclaimed with mock exuberance, 'The one in the officer's uniform, he's sooo handsome.'

Largo turned red. People saying the Captain was handsome irritated him. It seemed to miss the point, though quite which point this was, he was not sure.

'Yeah, us soldiers tend to get a lot of remarks like that,' he snapped back with his best attempt at weariness.

The girl looked closely at Largo.

'My, you *are* impatient,' she murmured, before adding quickly, 'You in particular, then, you get "a lot of that", do you?'

'I get enough,' Largo replied swiftly.

'And where,' the girl continued with a deliberate and lustful impertinence, 'do you get it?'

'Why don't you give him what he asked for, Muerta. Then tease him as much as you like,' the Captain's voice interjected.

The girl laughed aloud. 'Oh! how *severe*.'

The Captain came as close as his complexion would allow him to blushing, and looked down to Largo for help. Instead of seeing Largo, he saw stripes of yellow clay that had splattered his olive-green slacks. It looked, he feared, like he had been sick down his front.

'Don't you tease any more, Captain?' the girl enquired mockingly.

The Captain eyed the girl cautiously.

'I don't know anyone apart from you who teases any more,' he said, hoping that this would allow him to find a foothold.

Muerta Astro felt a gentle flush move over her and smiled. If she had been sober she would have probably enjoyed another laugh. Together Largo and the Captain made quite a pair, each falling hopelessly short of their self-image. Both stood in postures that were made all the more ridiculous if one knew, as Muerta did, that neither man had reached his twenty-second birthday. Moreover, both of them looked like miscast actors playing the part of soldiers, their true vocations being Matador and Pirate.

'What are you sighing for, Muerta?' the Captain asked tentatively.

'I didn't know I was sighing, but if I am it's because of you, you make me sigh,' she replied gaily.

'I expect you say that to all your men.'

'Oh, I wish!' she slurred coyly. 'Anyway, why were you ignoring me, like you always do, when you were standing over there?'

'I wasn't ignoring you, I just didn't think you'd want to say hello to me,' said the Captain, allowing his shoulders to relax and drop.

'Not say hello to you? Silly boy!' Muerta giggled, happy that the Captain had not asked why she had been reduced to working in a beer stall at a co-operative fair.

Clicking her tongue, Muerta rolled down her apron and climbed over the plank separating her from him.

The Captain could tell by her assertive but clumsy movements that she was drunk and would, one day, forget everything they were about to do together.

Walking right up to the Captain, Muerta stopped, performed a hundred-and-eighty-degree turn, and, imitating a fainting nun, collapsed into his arms. Her figure had been boyish but had now developed curves; her eyes, less committed than the Captain remembered them, were still interested enough to laugh as she opened them.

'You've cut your hair again,' she whispered.

Breathing over the side of his neck, one hand running up his back, the other one creeping down his waist, Muerta began to sing a song she knew the Captain liked.

A few yards away Ali turned to Josip and, looking down at the boy a few inches shorter than himself, smiled awkwardly. 'You used to go out with her, didn't you?'

'There are a lot of things in life that you just have to accept,' Josip replied, making Ali wonder whether he had actually heard the question properly.

Largo, having helped himself to a tray of beers, grunted and started towards where the others were standing, careful to avoid the lake-like puddles as he went. As he passed Muerta, balanced in the arms of the

Captain, he caught a memorable glimpse of her ample, but contained, breasts. A sight his memory would be able to dissect more fully later.

It was Ali who picked him up out of the mud.

'I'm sorry. I didn't see the rope,' Largo spluttered. 'The beers are all over the place, look, I'll get . . .'

'Relax, we didn't need eight anyway. You should watch where you're going. I'll get this round, you go and see if one of those girls will lend you a set of clothes. You're a mess.'

Largo's breathing slowed down and his face returned to its normal colour of yellow and pink oils.

'Thanks, Ali.'

'Here, Josip, you take him.'

Picking him up, Ali passed Largo to Josip, who lifted the dwarf on to his shoulders, securing a better view of the action on stage. Largo fixed his eyes on the girl he had spotted earlier, who, at that moment, was crawling through the legs of the girl with long legs and beautiful eyes. It was hard to decide which of the two he preferred so, diplomatically, he opted to love them both.

The other girls, with slices of apple jammed in the folds of their lips, had formed a triangle in which each took turns to dive under the arms of the others, with every third girl snatching the apple from under the lips of every first. To the spectator it seemed like a private and exotic children's game. Old men sat either side of the stage playing the folk music that was unique to the region and, behind them, rows of middle-aged men stood singing in the posture of pining men. Outside the tent, in which Muerta Astro lay with the Captain, the girls seemed deaf to the songs of these pining men, but for Largo the girls had knowledge; knowledge of why the men pined and why they would continue to do so.

'I can't believe it.'

The Captain could believe it only too well.

'I can't believe we did this again. I don't usually do it with the same person twice. Not once I've stopped seeing them, I mean.'

The Captain pulled Muerta Astro's trousers back up over her plump buttocks and stepped out of the tent into the night.

A crooked old man selling candles was moving around the edges of the crowd that had gathered in front of the stage. From a distance he reminded the Captain of Largo's father, Jarava Rollo, the mad old cobbler. Approaching him, he realised he was correct and greeted the old man loudly. 'Jarava, I can't believe I haven't seen you for so long. Where've you been hiding?' This sort of unforced joviality being typical of the Captain, once he had got his end away.

The old man, preferring not to reciprocate the warmth of the greeting, instead muttered thick gibberish beneath his breath. Like his son, he barely reached the Captain's shoulders.

'What's that you're saying?'

'This field.'

'What?'

'You, young man, be careful, don't sleep here, I've

spent plenty of nights here and I know. There are snakes in this field.'

'It sounds like there's more on your mind than you're able to say,' the Captain bawled happily, quite sure he was humouring a harmless old lunatic.

The old man didn't reply but moved his eyes so that they were level with the Captain's shoulders and, with both arms, saluted.

'Make sure my son knows of everything that's happened here.'

'I'm sorry?'

'Tell my son of everything you've heard here.'

Making a mental note not to, the Captain smiled, shook the old man's hand, bowed briefly and continued the walk across the field to his friends.

They were crowded around a heap of stacked-up crates, on their third or fourth beer. Behind them flares were being let off in the sky, and behind the flares grew the rising sound of gunfire. Discordant at first, then gradually becoming more rhythmic. For a moment the Captain felt as though he was about to experience himself as the subject of gossip. He walked up to the table. The men were quiet.

'Do you think Alcazar expects anyone to fire back?' asked Ali.

'That all depends on who you think he's firing at,' replied the Captain, standing some distance away so as to not give Ali the impression that there was time for another beer.

'Forget Alcazar, what have you done with Muerta?' Josip asked slowly, his expression neither mischievous nor serious.

'I don't know, I think she's probably where I left her,' the Captain opined feebly, cautious of perhaps having trodden on Josip's toes.

It was through Josip that the Captain had first met Muerta, though at the time it had not been made clear whether she was Josip's wife or girlfriend. Muerta was a history-less figure who, like Josip, had arrived in Catalonia during the great rural migration of the early thirties. The only thing that *was* clear about her was that Josip held her fidelity in no high regard and it did not take long for the Captain's knowledge of her to become intimate. She took little exception to being swapped between the two men intermittently, all the while claiming that she had them both where she wanted. This was, in fact, a lie, as Muerta could sustain no real interest in men, preferring instead to look forward to a career as an exotic belly-dancing star of the stage. Consequently, no man had ever demonstrated a consistent interest in Muerta, though the look in Josip's eyes told the Captain that this trend was in danger of changing.

Josip laughed at the Captain's sudden awkwardness and, without warning, launched into a monologue in the voice of a highly feminised Captain.

'I've told Muerta that if she fools around I'll leave her and that there's no point asking me not to because I'll have already made up my mind to go. So when I see her at a party, making out she's not interested in me, I'll call her over and tell her that it's over, that I've been pushed too far, that I think she's a whore and that's that. I'm too proud to be strung around like a lovesick prick.'

The Captain clutched his hand over his mouth in mock shock. He had always admired this absolutist streak in Josip. The monologue was one he remembered giving word for word at a party a few months earlier, and it was drunken trash that Josip had a good knack for remembering.

'Her trouble,' Josip concluded, continuing in the Captain's voice, 'is that she loves it and that the price she pays for loving it is everything else.'

'One all.' The Captain smiled, sympathetic enough to realise that Josip would not try to embarrass him if he did not, in his own peculiar way, love Muerta very much. It was a mistake to have taken Josip's simplicity at face value.

'And that's why you can't do anything for a woman like that,' Largo added keenly, oblivious to any ironic content in the conversation. 'They're like mad cats from bad homes . . .'

'I don't think this was intended as a free-for-all, Largo,' the Captain interjected.

Largo looked over to Josip for approval and support: Josip didn't stir, his gaze locked into something just behind his bottle of beer. For a redhead, Josip certainly had a long fuse, thought Largo, as he searched for something to say.

'You'd better make yourselves comfortable and then

get to the car. We're off again in five minutes,' said the Captain, taking advantage of the silence.

Largo and Ali got up and moved over towards a line of men relieving themselves over a stretch of hedge. Josip stayed where he was, slumped against a crate of wet and mouldy oranges.

'You enjoyed yourself, then?' he asked, his voice utterly serious in its hurt. The Captain looked Josip over carefully. It was possible that he was a little drunk, any alcohol he had just consumed being a top-up on what he'd enjoyed the night before, and the morning after that.

'Do you really feel that taken aback, Josip?' The Captain was genuinely surprised. Even if Josip was in pain it was unusual for him to not disguise it beneath his immense reserves of pride.

'Taken aback in what way?'

'Because of what's just happened between me and Muerta.'

'Oh no, anyone's welcome to swallow oysters with her for all I care. If I wanted it otherwise I would have made an honest women of her.'

'Josip, are you making fun of me?'

There was a pause as both men tried to work out how serious their misunderstanding was.

'Did your wife ever find out about you and her?' the Captain said in an attempt to widen the scope of the conversation, and give them both a way out.

'Not exactly. The wife thought Muerta was a log and that it was her sister I was after.'

'Were you?'

'Well, they were both beautiful, especially Muerta.'

'But how much *do* you actually like Muerta?' asked the Captain falteringly. This was a question he had never thought of asking before. 'Do you like her enough to think I've used her?'

'Well . . .' Josip stretched the word out as far as it would go. It was not a question he had ever thought of answering before, and he was not sure whether, through saving her honour, he could save his own too.

'I don't know if I do like her all that much.' The lie made his heart tilt to one side as he continued, 'I mean, I love her figure, but we're not exactly what you'd call friends.'

'So you don't think you and her have anything . . .' The Captain stopped and blew out of his mouth as if to search for the right word. '. . . have done anything together that will always mean something to both of you?'

'I don't know. I mean no. I have a family, you know that.'

'I wanted to make sure that I hadn't hurt you.'

'Well, you don't need to. Muerta has a way of turning from a bit of fun into a sour pint.'

The Captain nodded gratefully for this advice and the two men fell quiet.

Josip got up and together they walked back through the mud to the car.

Chapter Five

Muerta Astro drew heavily on what was left of her cigarette. She did not usually smoke, but since she already expected to wake up with a headache she had figured what the hell, and was now on her fifth cigarette of the evening. The air had started to feel significantly colder than it had an hour earlier, and she cursed herself for not having brought out warmer clothes. She knew it was a mistake to dress as if autumn nights would always be as hot as summer afternoons.

Seeking warmth, she walked over to where Jarava Rollo was balancing his hands over a forest of candles he had erected. He looked at her and blinked. Muerta returned his look with a smile; her evening was now over, and it seemed as sensible to sit with an old man as it had earlier to sleep with a young one.

'My son's a soldier,' rasped Jarava.

'I beg your pardon?'

'My son, Largo, he's a captain in the army,' Jarava repeated, with a little elaboration.

'You must be very proud of him,' Muerta answered sincerely.

'I am very proud of him. Look at all the medals he's given me.' Jarava tapped his breast.

'They're lovely,' Muerta cooed.

'Which of them do you like best?'

Muerta studied Jarava's chest carefully. She was not exactly sure what was expected of her in this exchange, but wanted to make the old man happy.

'That one.' She pointed. 'The one that looks like it's made of moonstone.'

Jarava unpinned the 'medal' and examined it under the candlelight. It was a large pastoral ring bound to a baby badger's skull by wire.

'Here, you have it,' he offered.

'Are you sure?' Muerta blushed. 'It's too beautiful to give away . . .'

Her words were interrupted by the approach of growling engines. A convoy of trucks was advancing up the bank towards the fair, led by an armoured car draped in the national flag. Two of the trucks had broken from the main column and were driving into the throng. Muerta froze, her mind at the mercy of word-of-mouth atrocities, and images of rape. Sick with fear, she drew herself up slowly and began to walk away from the string of lights surrounding the field.

The first person to be killed in the gunfire was Simon, who, having left Antonio, had been busy getting drunk a few crates away from where Largo and the others had been resting. He had watched Muerta Astro for the best part of an hour, noticed the confidence with which she had scratched her ass and swung her hips and, inspired by this, had tried to lodge his hand in the gap between her proud legs as she brushed past him.

Simon had not even been gratified with a response and quickly reconciled himself to the fact that there were men in the world who must mean more to Muerta than he did. Another drink banished lust but left him bruised and melancholic. His thoughts collapsed into a muddle, and only after much trying was he able to conclude that if he was not so given to useless reflection, he would enjoy more success with women. Encouraged by his new-found clarity, he shouted an obscenity at a girl he took to be Muerta. By the time he got to thinking of his wife, he had forgotten what he'd shouted and who it was who had paid for him to get drunk.

He was oblivious to the first bullet that arrived in his side with a muffled thud. The second bullet, flying through his hand, alerted him to the fact that he was being shot at, and, as the third bullet travelled through his gut, he remembered the civil war, that this was the civil war. Lying dying beneath the bench, Simon smiled. How much of this would he remember when he woke up?

A little over a mile away, Chyrysa, Simon's wife, watched Antonio Mayle back his car out of her drive. It was a year since they had last met and she was grateful that she still meant something to him, bearing in mind the other women he had probably been through since. The memories of their brief affair had kept her going, though, and they were far from exhausted. The memory of Antonio climbing over her wall and losing one of his shoes, the memory of their trip to the sea, where he had bought her ice cream (she had interpreted it as a sign of love; he had probably forgotten why he had even done it), but above all the active memory of their sex. How he held her as it happened and how she had felt afterwards. Their interaction had been incredible, but sadly tempered by the absence of a very wide yardstick through which Chyrysa might measure her pleasure. She had only ever had one other partner – Simon.

She sneered with force, and imagined her husband standing in front of her.

There was no comparison between the two men.

Locking the front door, she walked back into the house and buried her face in the underpants Antonio had thoughtfully left her. Simon would have to let himself in.

The Perez-Barabo fair had become a long series of explosions flanked, on all sides, by the tangled remains of trucks and other machinery. Colonel Raul Alcazar, hidden in the remains of the main stage, ran a finger along his life-line and reviewed the situation. The most important thing now was to prevent his popularity being damaged any further by allowing any more of his men to be killed. And the second most important thing was to avoid getting more mud on his clothes.

The battle had not enjoyed an auspicious start. His

men, who had somehow allowed a whole column of nationalists to bypass their roadblock, had arrived unprepared and been made to pay. More irritatingly, the engagement bore all the signs of being costly in terms of lives, but, unlike the set-piece battles taking place around Madrid, militarily quite insignificant.

'Sir! There's a machinegun still operational behind that truck.'

'Which truck are you talking about?' Three or four of the vehicles lay jammed at the point at which the road became a mud track. 'On the other side of that fallen tree.' His second-in-command pointed.

'I still can't see what you're talking about,' hissed Alcazar, pressing his grime-caked binoculars closer to his face. The range he was operating at made them unnecessary, but, since he had lost his spectacles farther up the road, the binoculars were serving as a useful psychological crutch.

'There, sir, the fire's coming from over there!'

'That's not a machinegun,' Alcazar spat contemptuously, 'it's concentrated heavy rifle fire!'

A shell flew across the field, hitting what structure survived of the stage and knocking the whole edifice into a burning wicker man.

'That's not the work of a rifle, sir, they must have a tank with them.'

'Give me back the field glasses.'

Another shell banged high over Alcazar's head. The distance comforted him; they were firing wide.

'They should have spent more time at the target

range. At this sort of distance they should be making mincemeat of us . . .'

A third shell landed a few feet away from Alcazar, sending a large clod of earth sailing through the air. Their marksmanship was improving quickly.

'What the hell were you thinking of when you let that disaster through our roadblock?' Alcazar shrieked involuntarily. His second-in-command blushed, his left arm hanging in shreds from a shattered shoulder.

'I'm sorry. In the dark they must have looked like ours . . .'

The man's voice was broken by the weight of another explosion.

Alcazar came to a moment later amongst a cluster of ripe corn. For a minute it felt like he was in heaven but, because of the noise, it quickly became apparent that he was not; that heaven was what he was look-ing up at, and earth was where he was trapped. His second-in-command had landed inches away from him and fallen like a ripe apple. Alcazar watched the man's organs empty out of his open gut as either side of them flames raced across the tops of the burning corn piles.

'Everything always falls to pieces whenever I turn my back,' Alcazar mumbled grimly, as if to confirm he was still alive. Feeling both his arms and legs return to him, he rolled on to his belly and refocused his attention on the light aircraft gun that had now moved into the open. From its new position it was busy wreaking havoc at combatant and non-combatant alike. The gun crew's attention had been caught by a line of dancing girls running towards the comparative safety of the woods. Within seconds a yard-long flame licked from the gun's muzzle, catching the girls in its path. Reloading hastily, without pausing to clear the barrel of the wet earth stuck in it, the crew fired again, this time finding themselves their own target, the air reeling with their screams, peppered in the shattered muzzle of their own weapon. This was the sort of break Alcazar had waited for and he knew that he would have to take advantage of it. The field was still awash with small-arms fire, making a frontal assault dangerous at best, but, led by deranged impatience, Alcazar sprung to his feet and yelled at the top of his voice, 'Everyone at once, follow me!'

His men, scattered as they were, caught the mood of his fury and, rising in groups, followed him into battle. Rather than holding their position, the enemy, as Alcazar had predicted, rushed out to meet them, moving with the eagerness of men who enjoy war. The battle, faster than either side had expected, became hand to hand with some men dropping off in surprise at the logical outcome of their aggression. Elsewhere men fell around in the mud, jabbing and goading each other without really wishing to get involved in the fighting.

Alcazar, far ahead of the rest of his men, now fell into the path of a giant twice his size. Both men stopped inches before collision and ran their eyes over each other's uniforms. Alcazar reached for his knife but the man, acting faster, swung the point of his spade round, knocking them both off balance. From his place on the ground, Alcazar kicked wildly at the giant's face and, thinking clearly through his panic, lunged at the man's body, lodging his knife in the groin and cutting upwards. Behind him his men, inspired by his example, hacked into the enemy with the same malicious energy, chasing them back into their own covering fire. Three or four stood their ground, shouting at others to do the same and flailing blindly as if in a fist fight, but far more dropped their weapons and pleaded to be taken prisoner, as those who did not were cut down.

Beginning at point-blank range, Alcazar began to pick off the enemy wounded; the contest was all but over. A long and conjoined roar had started to spread across the field. It was the sound of his men cheering. Less than a third of his company had been wounded in the fighting and only four killed.

'Give me a minute.'

Alcazar drained the dregs of a jug of milk and cast his eyes over what remained of the enemy.

'Who are these people?'

'We don't know, they've got no pay-books. I should think they're an irregular outfit.'

Alcazar caught the eye of one man a little taller than the others, clad in a decorated uniform of the old regime. He knew at once that he was about to address a fanatic, a dispossessed landowner, or a colonel whose politics lost him his rank; either way, though, a fanatic.

'You in the pyjamas, get out in front where I can count how many badges you have,' Alcazar yelled mockingly.

The man stepped out slowly, with controlled dignity, and stared over his captors' heads as though they were not there. Despite his regal stance, it was obvious that he was uncomfortable with this latest turn in his fortunes. His discomfort was not eased by the way the ground that separated him from Alcazar was occupied by the body of a bargirl – her abdomen perforated with bullets – that his men had left there. His eyes twitched nervously; it was probably useless trying to convince anyone of the rectitude of his actions, but, and this was the point, he had nothing to lose. Wiping a line of blood from under his nose, the injured man turned to his captors and snarled, 'You think you're soldiers but you're not even a proper army, you're just paid killers for a government that shouldn't exist. None of you have ever known what it's like to wear a uniform that actually means something. Not you, "Colonel", and not any of your men.' Breathing deeply, the man continued with increased confidence: 'Don't any of you ever hear or see something that makes you want to get up and say, "I love this country and I'll defend everything she does and stands for . . ."'

The man never got to finish his speech. One by one, he and the rest of his men were taken to the nearby wood and hanged. The spectacle was watched, at a distance, by Antonio Mayle, happy that his car was still roadworthy and even firmer in his conviction that politics was best left to the enthusiasts. In his passenger seat Muerta Astro wiped the dirt out of her wound.

Chapter Six

It had been a quiet night at the temporary headquarters of Army Group C. From an open window, at the far end of the main parade ground, a thin man, whose knowledge of life extended no farther than the commands he issued, shouted another order. Within seconds the surface of the courtyard below was packed with other voices, the fast rhythm of their chatter led by panic, its suppressed volume a symptom of misplaced respect for their commander.

The man at the window slowly rocked his head in approval at what he saw and turned to his next challenge. 'I'm sorry, but there is nothing more that can be done for him now, and, if you're as astute as I think you are, you'll treat him as though he were already dead. I'm sorry but there you are, that's the way it is.'

The man cleared his throat and growled happily before continuing, 'You see, it's not as if we're dealing with what, at the end of the day, is a matter that can be understood vis-à-vis the apparatus of personal considerations, far from it, what we are facing here is a situation in which everyone loses something. They lose one of theirs, so we lose one of ours. It is as simple and, not to put too fine a point on it, as brutal, as that. Of course, given the choice, I would rather the world was a different place but, as I'm sure you'll agree, that's the sort of thing theologians deal with. I'm a soldier and I take things as I find them.'

The man trailed off as a separate series of thoughts, as yet unconnected, floated just outside his expressive range.

'Look at it like this,' he began again, 'sometimes I look down there at our boys, each setting about his own business, and I say to myself . . .'

'I don't care about your boys. If I had wanted to talk about them I'd have visited a . . .' an impatient listener interrupted.

'I look at our boys out there and there are times, I won't deny that there aren't, when they appear to me to be just bodies and not men, but as soon as that sort of thought enters my mind I'm rid of it, I get a grip, I remind myself who they are, what they mean to me and what they are doing.'

The man allowed himself an embarrassed smile, as if to admit he was not really sure what he was talking about or where this analogy was leading to.

'How do you know that they are not just bodies?'

'Because I get a grip. And besides, if you would allow me to return to the point, it would be helpful for you to think of Braulio Rojo in that way from now on too, as just a body. I'm sorry if I seem to contradict myself but my point is that sometimes, whatever a person may mean to you, it is best just to regard them as a body to be acted on. In this life there is no other way to get things done.'

The man stopped, twitched, and, quite suddenly, reached an arm out to the man he was addressing, who had, as suddenly, bent down and covered his face.

The man who had been doing the listening was Dr Ernesto Rojo, brother of the Don and son of Carla Rojo, the family's matriarch. The man who had been talking was General Enrico Salazar-Rojo, Ernesto and the Don's half-brother. Holding Ernesto tightly with his arm, Salazar muttered a few barely audible words of regret.

'You see, it's what our left and their right want, old man, a blood exchange, a murderous blood exchange, and there's nothing to be done, understand me, nothing. Don Rojo, our beloved brother, is already as good as dead.'

These words of 'regret' were typical of Salazar, displaying, as they did, his theatrical contempt for sincerity and its attendant emotions.

'Dear boy, I have tried, believe me I have, *I have tried everything*, to stop things getting to this point, but . . .'

Angered by his brother's mendacious tone, Ernesto straightened his gait and unlocked himself from Salazar's half-embrace.

'I can't stay here with this going on, feeling like this and knowing what's going to happen, I should leave.'

'What do you mean?' Salazar threw his brother a sympathetic look and held out a hand.

Ernesto frowned and edged away slightly.

'Come on, Ernesto, this isn't like you, if there's something else you want say then get it out in the open.'

Salazar was right, it *was* uncharacteristic of Ernesto to make a stand even if the subject matter of their conversation was the projected murder of their elder brother, Don Rojo. If events had followed their normal course, Ernesto's slavish urge to be beaten down by his younger brother would have taken hold, and he would still be in Salazar's arm lock. Why Ernesto should have taken such perverse pleasure in deferring to a lesser man than himself was a mystery to everyone but the Don. The Don recognised that his brother's desire to subjugate himself before the strong was a temptation peculiar to the very intelligent and the very weak. In resisting Ernesto's attempts to worship him as a child, the Don had left the way open for their half-brother, Salazar, who had no such qualms in becoming the object of Ernesto's idolisation. Unfortunately Salazar did not possess any of the Don's worthier qualities, and was therefore forced to settle for Ernesto's obedience, rather than his love or respect. This had produced a tolerable state of affairs that remained unchallenged so long as Salazar never attempted to turn Ernesto, in mind or practice, against the Don.

Clearing his throat slightly desperately, Salazar grabbed Ernesto's wrist, determined to put an end to what he hoped was still just a misunderstanding.

'Now look here, don't you think you've left it a little late for . . .'

'He's our brother, Salazar, not just another person we think we know quite well, but our brother, our whole life.'

'What, our whole life for now or for ever?' Salazar shouted impulsively – his voice in its true element now – maddened at Ernesto's self-righteousness and keen to re-establish his natural dominance over what was fast developing into a slave revolt.

Ernesto raised his head so that he was looking straight into Salazar's eyes, able, from this angle, to check the strength of his half-brother's cynicism, which, he was relieved to discover, was flimsier than he had expected. Salazar, realising eye contact had been made, broke it off immediately and turned to the window, his whole body shaking with anger. Perhaps, Ernesto wondered, beneath those curls of blond hair, ribbons and self-confidence, Enrico Salazar was not a man used to being tested.

'I'm leaving now.'

Salazar, still shaking, said nothing, thus emboldening Ernesto even further.

'I think, Salazar,' Ernesto said slowly, deliberately taking time over his words to check the extent of his new-found resolve, 'I think the way you've talked about this, and your reasons for wanting it done, are not right.'

Salazar, seemingly a different man from the one he was a moment earlier, turned around and nodded guiltily, his eyes disturbed by their sudden discovery of tears.

'Look, no one knows me better than you, Ernesto . . . I wouldn't say the things I do if I really thought about them. My God! If I did really think before I spoke I probably wouldn't say anything at all! That's the real difference between me and Braulio, he's a thinker who talks and I'm a doer who thinks . . .'

Ernesto sighed inwardly at the terrible aphorism and shook his head. Salazar's body had not been shaking with anger or emotion but with momentary confusion. The lapse, however, was now over and he was back to his bullshitting best.

'. . . and you know that's not all that stands between us. For example, if I'm given a problem I'll see if I can solve it. Now, if that was Braulio in the same situation, solving the problem would be the last thing he would do. He'd want to think through the problem, approach it from all the different angles, see every side to it . . .'

'The difference between you and Braulio is that he might not be happy with who he is but you don't even know who you are. You won't even do anything to help me save his life, for God's sake.'

'I've told you, there's nothing I can do.' Salazar's tone had reverted to that of the military man angry at being interrupted mid-flow. 'I've been deliberately kind over this to protect your feelings and my own, but we both know this has got nothing to do with tit-for-tat revenge and everything to do with Braulio's proposed defection. And there's only one way that can end.'

'That's it, is it?'

'Yes, that is it.'

'I can't believe you mean it. You'll change your mind and see sense but by then it'll be too late. You *must* do something now.'

Salazar turned around to face the window again.

'Think about the consequences of this, Salazar . . .' Ernesto felt the words stop and fall out of his mouth. He had often wondered what it would feel like if something that was once held to be precious *changed*; when a husband could no longer speak to his wife of thirty years or where one old friend could no longer look the other in the eye. What had struck him as absurd about these situations was how quickly a shared past became obsolete in the face of a new reality that cared nothing for it. How human it was to finally become the man who shouts, 'How can you not want to talk to me, *we woke up next to each other* for thirty years,' knowing all the while that whatever had allowed him to make up with her had already passed through his hands.

Ernesto shook his head, running his thumb across his moustache. If there was a chance of saving this situation it would not be through the efforts of Enrico Salazar because, and this was what he had failed to understand until now, something had *changed*.

For both men, the point of the meeting had dissolved into an unpleasant exchange which, though unsettling, felt unreal. Ernesto picked his hat off the table and, without properly acknowledging his brother, left the room. In truth Salazar was right. Neither of them held any illusions over the Don's encroaching martyrdom. Deceit and deception had become necessary conditions in each of their lives and it was just the Don's bad luck to have projected too far ahead, and left himself inadequately covered for the present.

Ernesto walked across the courtyard to the stables where he had tied up his horse. Breathing in the scent of the damp hay, he felt more himself, but his conscience was still bound up with the Don's fate. Something the Don had told him years ago made him laugh and, Ernesto thought, would make the Don laugh too, if he knew how thin the tightrope of bitten string had become. It had followed the death of a bullfighter they had both admired. 'How is it that the clowns always survive and the key players end up dead?' the Don had asked.

Ernesto looked up at the night. Nothing had changed.

11.15 p.m. – the Rojo hacienda

Lucille checked her watch. She could do nothing until he arrived. She checked her watch again – neither hand had moved significantly. Turning on her heels, she began the walk from her porch to the end of the drive for the sixth time that evening. Each walk was counted and classed in a set of three and, if there was no sign of Antonio by the time she reached the twenty-first set of three, she would finally *do* something about this relationship, which was always as young as its last argument.

Above her, the sky changed colour again, from black to a dim phosphorous yellow, a result, though she did not know it, of the exploding anti-aircraft gun at the fair. The night had already provided several distractions over the past hour – the sound of distant music, thunderclaps, even the high-pitched screams of those caught between dying and death. Noisy as each of these agents of an external world were, none carried the requisite force to divert Lucille from her number game. Her interest in the bigger picture was intense but inconsistent, the gap between her feelings and her feelings for the world too large for any real dialogue between the two spheres. Perhaps this was why it didn't strike her that the background noise of the world could have had a bearing on why Antonio had failed to turn up, and on why she was playing a number game instead of riding in the passenger seat of his car.

Sitting in the doorway to the house, Rosa Rojo, a few inches shorter and a few pounds heavier than her sister, tried to wish herself into her Lucille's shoes. That this process was saturated with jealousy was clear enough. Rosa would have exchanged everything for the excitement of knowing that, at any minute, a man on whom everything depended could turn into the drive and sound the horn for her. Lucille, however, viewed neither waiting nor her partner in these exalted terms. It was stoicism, not excitement, that kept her going and provided the necessary balance that kept her imaginative powers in check. Without such stoicism her ability to experience possibility as something that had actually happened, and to confuse this for truth, would have undoubtedly driven her mad. The reality of the hypothetical (Antonio dying in a car crash, Antonio finding another woman on the way to her house) was still powerful enough to temporarily engulf her (even now, renegade thoughts were mushrooming into thousands of questionable scenarios), but stoicism, though unable completely to annul her fears, at least taught her to care less about them. If Antonio were to turn up immediately, blaming his unpunctuality on a flat tyre, she would not be surprised, nor would it surprise her if he did not turn up at all. In minutes it would be decided, a single event would either confirm or kill the imagination that had attempted to prophesy it, and Lucille would know the number and nature of any fresh injuries.

Turning around, she started the walk back to the porch, her movements slower now, slower because she realised that reaching the seventh set of three would change nothing, that her numbering system would simply continue to expand until the arrival of its goal, Antonio. Perhaps her father was right and love was like politics; that reality tended towards a compromise of interests and only the painful extremes of her mind were at fault for thinking reality was more horrible, and subsequently richer, than it actually was. But even if this were true, and it was a mistake to live as though the single most disturbing explanation for something was always correct, it was equally foolish to believe that the disturbing was necessarily false. To some extent, Lucille reasoned, it depended on who you were and how much reason you had to fear the disturbing, how close your relationship was to panic and how comfortable you felt with the unpredictable. Gulping nervously, she tried to turn her mind back towards the numbering game.

'Lucille.'

'Yes!'

'It's the telephone, for you.'

Pulling up her tights and lowering her dress, Lucille glanced at her reflection in the window of her father's car; she was striking and demure, more or less the way she appeared in photographs. Brushing past her sister, and forgetting to sound calm, she grabbed the phone.

At the Third Army emergency call booth, just over a mile away, the Captain hung up.

The line went dead.

'What did he say?' called Rosa.

'Nothing,' snorted Lucille.

She was allowing herself to be treated like an idiot's pet; it was something everyone knew but it was the first time she had realised it this clearly for herself. Antonio may have enjoyed a certain self-image of laid-back cool and, in a rather crude way, a sense of humour, but that was as far as things went. Despite what her sister said, her feelings for Antonio did not run deep. His dashing-bastard persona bored and irritated her in equal measure, and, once the talking was done with, he had proved to be a bad kisser. This, and the fact that his low resistance to alcohol had led him to call her a proud bitch, ensured that it was her pride, and not her heart, that was affected by his treatment of her.

'So it was him!' her sister said gleefully. 'You can always recognise Antonio's voice on the telephone.'

'If it was he's behaving like a complete prick to me.'

'Everyone's a prick to you if they're not at your beck and call.'

Feeling too angry to tell her sister how wrong she was, Lucille returned, with grim inevitability, to the now familiar image of her and Antonio undressed. Their last attempt at sex had been miserable. Having failed to compliment what she assumed to be Antonio's standard repertoire, the two had moved on and off one another listlessly until Antonio had accused her of frigidity, bringing the exchange, and its attendant awkwardness, to an end. Worse still, this return to semi-carnality destroyed the pleasant associations that existed for her between the sexual act and the past. Her memory of previous intimacies belonged to a different part of her brain from that which she used, to blot out her current dip in luck. The most vivid of these memories was of a morning partly informed by sleep and partly by touch. She and the Captain had woken up together not as people but as architecture, and, depending on how he held her, as a large house, built of white stone, with three walls and a garden. This strange mood had lasted well into the afternoon, by which time the two had become newly built towns, each reliant on the industry of the other. These were hours that nothing existed either side of, saved in memory and qualified through time.

Lucille picked at a tooth. Was it possible that the boy she had once been so sure of was now someone else, someone she had been right to reject in the effort to make herself anew? It was a question she was reluctant to answer. For if there was one thing she enjoyed now, or at least tried to, it was her newly found strength, and she would never allow falling in love to deprive her of it again.

She looked at her watch. Antonio was over two hours late.

Antonio withdrew from Muerta, stuffed a handful of notes into her mouth and pushed her out of the passenger seat.

'There goes your money's worth,' he muttered through his breath. The expression was one he was fond of using; it could always act as a concise summary of events.

Muerta winced, scraping the money out of her mouth. Its taste was ashen and powdery. Waving it in the air, she yelled, 'Is this your way of telling me you love me, *Stud*?'

Not wishing to discuss the point, Antonio started his engine, drowning out Muerta's volley of curses. Adjusting his pants and straightening his seat, he veered his car back on to the main road, shouted, 'In your eye, pissface,' and joined a long convoy of trucks on their way to the front.

Left behind again and without a lift into town, Muerta Astro held on to the money, unsure whether to keep it or not. The wound in her arm where the shrapnel had landed hardly hurt at all, but her pride had taken a hell of a battering. Was indiscriminate promiscuity a phase in life, or would it be like this for ever? Either way, it had not been a night she would one day tell her children about.

Tucking the money into her belt, Muerta emitted a long sigh. As expected, no one heard.

Chapter Seven

11.45 p.m. – the Perez-Baroba fair

Raul Alcazar had not been hard to find; the lines of smoke emanating from the Perez-Baroba fair were thick enough to give his position away to Ernesto Rojo, who had ridden as fast as he could through the stretch of woodland that separated the battle-strewn field from the headquarters of Army Group C. The ride had been pleasant; the smell of damp leaves had mixed with the aroma of burning wood, reminding Ernesto of the bonfires that he, the Don and Salazar had built as boys. Only the sound of low moaning from the edges of the wood, and what looked like, but could not be, the silhouettes of men hanging in bunches from the surrounding trees, warned Ernesto that he had not undertaken this ride for pleasure.

Alcazar's greeting had not been ceremonious. 'I think the cracks are appearing.' Alcazar pointed to his men. 'If I don't let them rest now they'll have changed sides by morning.'

Ernesto Rojo could tell that neither imagination nor empathy were informing his old friend's judgment, but rather the experience of shared exhaustion. But Raul Alcazar was his last hope and, unlike

Salazar, was not a man who had been much changed by adulthood.

'Raul, I'm not asking for your whole company, just for enough men to guard the gates and doors of Braulio's hacienda. He needs help now like he's never needed it before.'

Alcazar yawned loudly. The perspiration lining his clothes had dried, giving him an increased sense of physical discomfort. Ernesto, in marked contrast, looked like he was ready to begin the day at his doctor's practice, his panama jacket and jodhpurs still pressed and creased, bearing only the slightest signs of freshly splattered mud. Of the three Rojo brothers this was the only one Alcazar still regarded as a friend but, knowing him well enough to know that he did not own a temper, he felt little inclination to do as he asked.

'I'm sorry, Ernesto, but I've had enough of tonight. We're going to have to leave this for another time.'

'We can't.'

'I can.' Alcazar smiled sleepily. 'Come back and bother me in a few hours and maybe I'll have the strength to talk to you.'

Alcazar bent down and arranged his pack so as to make a pillow of it.

'Raul! In a few hours my brother will be dead and . . .'

Ernesto was talking in vain; Alcazar was already flat on his back, his cap pulled over his face. All around them his men were starting to do the same thing.

Ernesto remembered only one other occasion on

which Raul Alcazar seemed so close to total collapse. This was years earlier, during their first semester at the Academy. Raul had come through the tail-end of the mother of all benders, the cause on this occasion being the girl who would, in a different incarnation, become his second wife. This development seemed far from apparent at the time, and the young Alcazar, having drunk several tankards of cider and taken leave of his senses, attempted to end his own life. His success was fortunately limited to a gash on the forehead and the destruction of his father's outside toilet, in which he had been held captive for his own safety. If Alcazar could listen to his past now, Ernesto reflected, he would hear it laugh at him.

Alcazar, for his part, was quite at home in his immediate environment. His subtler thoughts, and their accompanying comforts, had, until a moment ago, been eclipsed by a swarm of itches and pangs, ranging from mosquito bites to wet feet. But these, in turn, had calmed, allowing Alcazar to lower himself gently into the gratifying peace of a deep sleep.

They say I am in love with words but I hate them.

They say I court society but I am bashful.

They say I love other women when you know you are the only woman I have ever known and loved.

They were only right about my arrogance, which was easily got rid of and easy to reacquire.

They say I am in love with . . .

'Braulio, let whatever it is go, let yourself sleep.'

The Don felt his back float over the cold surface of sweat that rose from his sheets. He closed his eyes. The sleep sounds that were working through him had stopped. New sounds were emerging and for once they were all making the same noise:

You don't know anyone until you have played their part.

'Have we come here for the same thing?' the old woman asked, her voice betraying an anxiety that bordered on anger.

'I've come to see if my son's still alive,' replied her neighbour in the queue.

'Why shouldn't he be?'

'He was at the fair earlier, he rides with those irregulars just like your son, I'm afraid that . . .'

'Bless him, he looks so peaceful when he's resting,' interrupted a soldier, pointing at Alcazar's snoring body.

It was true, Raul Alcazar resembled nothing so much as a satisfied baby when asleep.

'And you expect me to admire him for that?' muttered the nervous woman.

'You're lucky you're not buried with your son's victims, Mother Hen,' the soldier spat back contemptuously, and raised his arm as if to strike the old woman across the face.

Silently she lowered her head and gave up her place in the queue.

*   *   *

Raul Alcazar was having a more troubled sleep than his inertia suggested. His internal cinema was in the process of playing out an all too familiar nightmare.

Once again he was dreaming of a slow ascent towards heaven, the war on earth continuing without him. His journey up through its gates was neither smooth nor reassuring, but, for reasons he could not understand yet, as troubled as the life he had left behind. On his arrival he was transformed into a cruel caricature of himself, as he discovered that the war would continue here after all, that he was not in heaven but in hell. Remonstrating with the Devil, as he did on every other trip he made to this place, Alcazar repeated the same plea:

'Satan, please give me more time with my wife and children.'

As usual the Devil refused to listen. The cinema screen had become an old gramophone record, its slow and heavy sound moving like an iron hoof across Alcazar's sleeping soul.

He was woken by the cold air drifting across his face. It felt strangely pleasant. Above him Ernesto Rojo was chewing frantically at his nails and staring at him in an unnerving manner.

'So, Ernesto, what was it that you wanted to talk about?'

12.00 a.m. – the Buena Ventura monastery

General Salazar's self-perception was shaken, his confidence undercut. This was the fault of the unsettling exchange he had had with his half-brother, Ernesto Rojo, and the impression it had left on him. The impression being that it now took orders for people to obey him and do as he wanted. He remembered that in the past he was as persuasive as the Devil and that, in theory, the formal powers he now enjoyed as a general in the army were unnecessary. That this was no longer the case was precisely because his confidence had leant so heavily on these formal powers. They allowed him to cut corners, pre-empt useless arguments and, ultimately, to breathe. This enabled him to exercise a conversational freedom few men could enjoy. What unsettled him about this was the bully's paradox, the thought of people obeying his orders just because they would be shot or imprisoned if they did not. This was made even worse by the fact that Salazar had a curious relationship to his own orders, often issuing ones that he did not entirely agree with and yet drawing a perverse satisfaction from watching them being applied meticulously. His last order was of this type, the order to kill the Don, his half-brother.

'Sir.'

'Haven't you learned to knock before entering the room of a senior officer?'

'I'm sorry, sir, but I thought these reports that have just come in would be of some interest.'

Salazar rocked on his chair, his eyes disinterestedly skimming over the report. There had been some fighting at a 'religious' festival and the infantry had made a swine's arse of things, the event seeming to have ended up in a massacre of sorts. Big deal. In the end a report like this would only have been of interest if it had prevented his car returning from Nou Camp, and if that had happened he would have already known about it, so these reports, he concluded, were shit.

'Cresto, don't bother me in future unless you have something of real interest for me to read.'

'I am sorry, sir, but I thought you might have a personal interest in the role played by Raul Alcazar.'

Salazar returned his attention to the report, this time gazing at it carefully.

'So!' he snorted. 'Alcazar is still playing the medal game.' Reading aloud, he continued, 'Colonel Raul Alcazar, personally leading the counter-attack against well-fortified enemy positions! Well, who would have believed it at his age!'

'With all due respect, sir, it was you who rejected his application for a staff job at Nou Camp.'

Salazar ignored his subordinate and allowed his thoughts to range over the subject of Raul Alcazar. It pleased him to know that his old sparring partner was still out there, breaking iron in the night. The thought even made him chuckle inwardly. Even so, Alcazar still puzzled him. He had never quite been able to work him out, and for a long time he had erroneously believed they both had a lot in common. On finding out that they did not, the General's interest had turned into caution. It was best to leave soldiering to the soldiers.

'General, the reports have come in with the request

that Colonel Raul Alcazar be promoted back to the rank of acting Commander-in-Chief of the UGT battalions.'

'Commander-in-Chief, eh?' Salazar paused for a moment. Yes, acting Commander-in-Chief was fair enough. Alcazar, as untrustworthy as he was, was still preferable to the donkeys usually promoted to that rank.

Salazar countersigned the order.

'Cresto.'

'Yes, General?'

'Have my car ready to leave for Nou Camp at once, and I mean at once. That's an order.'

Don Rojo's eyes concentrated on the clock. Slowly he differentiated between its hands and, on finding out what time it was, groaned. There was still a long way to go until morning and there was little chance of him getting back to sleep. Turning slowly so as to not disturb his snoring wife, the Don edged off his side of the bed and reached for his dressing gown. For a minute or two he groped about in the dark, gently running one hand along the edge of his bedside table. Unable to find the gown, and unsure of what to do once he had got it on, the Don hauled himself up quietly and rubbed his eyes. Normally, with his sight accustomed to the dark, moving around was unproblematic, but tonight his body was not behaving in its usual way.

Beginning to feel the cold, the Don returned to the centre of the bed and started to readjust himself around his wife's body. What irritated him most at points like this was the frustration with oneself that accompanies the failure to fall asleep. He would have to circumnavigate this problem before it really got under way, and drove him completely mad. If it was possible to get warm enough in the next few minutes, he reasoned, then the sleeping process would probably take care of itself. Carefully he prised the covers from under his wife's back and dug them into a bottle-neck around his ankles and knees. Within seconds of his securing this position, his wife, purring lovingly, had settled on his chest, tugging the sheets back over her legs. Cursing the whole situation, the Don got back up, this time indifferent to the noise he was making, and defiantly strode towards the door.

'Better wrap up if you're going out for a walk,' murmured his wife.

The Don walked on, proud in his state of complete undress.

Helena Rojo moved to her husband's side of the bed and began to fiddle with the lamp. The phone call earlier in the evening had bothered her and, in contrast to every other threat the Don had received since the phone had been installed, there was something about this one that felt different. Or perhaps she only felt that way because she cared about her husband with a paranoia that bordered on obsession. She pulled the sheets up over her shoulders. The thought, and its apparent contradictions, was making her tired again, and she gave up trying to find the lamp and turned over to sleep.

*   *   *

General Salazar picked up his coat and straightened the knot in his tie. The worst thing about his rivalry with the Don, which, as far as he was concerned, had lasted for at least twenty-five years, was that he was never sure if the Don actually knew it existed. If asked who his main rivals were, the Don would probably laugh and claim to have none. If pressed he may have alluded to a certain amount of friendly duelling with Lazaro Itarable, leader of the right wing of the party, and perhaps to just a few light jousts with Angel Fejardo-Mendieta, former leader of the communist youth movement. And if the Don were really pushed he would finally concede, on a personal level, to never having had time for Inocente Conchoso, his regional party boss, and to having been antagonised by Raul Alcazar, commander of the Tereul garrison, since his schooldays, but it would have taken him a long time to reach the name of Enrico Salazar, two-star General and his half-brother.

Enrico Salazar, alone amongst the three brothers, had been adopted, his real parents remaining unknown, and of no interest to him since, in contrast to the disposition of his brothers, questions of origin and causation held no power over his imagination. He was, in this sense, very much a child of the here and now. People who were not, who were disposed towards either reflection or projection, were divided, by Salazar, between those he could afford to feel contempt for and those he was envious of. The Don fell within the latter category. Salazar found himself wanting, for as long as he was aware of wanting anything at all, the Don to finally fall flat on his face and fail at something he turned his hand to.

Unfortunately for Salazar, this ambition remained frustrated as the Don's life travelled along in a sequence of successes, each of his major life projects being executed with smug ease and style. Salazar was thus forced to content himself with smaller satisfactions, the size of which were pathetic to behold. For example, only a month earlier the Don had complained about the dreams he was experiencing. He was, he claimed, suffering from a barren patch, with those dreams he could remember not being worth the effort of being dreamt of in the first place. Salazar had had trouble concealing his delight. Not only did he find the Don's habit of pontificating about his dreams at length unbearably pompous and dull, but the exercise drummed home the point that Salazar, if he had dreams (which he didn't), would have been able to make a much better job of holding forth on them than the Don did. More irritatingly, but still wholly true to form, the Don had rung Salazar a week later telling him that the situation was saved. Not only was the Don dreaming again, but he could now remember all the dreams he'd thought he had never had during his 'barren patch'. And they had been *marvellous*.

Salazar could still taste the bile in his mouth.

Having locked the door to his office, he made his

way down into the courtyard, taking his steps deliberately slowly in order to maintain the regal air he
believed his men expected of him. The courtyard, and
the buildings surrounding it, had only recently been
turned to military uses. Salazar's first experience of
them, thirty years earlier, had been as a schoolboy
attending the Jesuit seminary that they were built to
accommodate. He and the Don had stood together
in front of the headmaster, Father Torriente, in what
was now Salazar's office, and been told that they
would both be suspended for straying out of school
bounds the night before. Father Torriente, certainly
not the strictest priest at the seminary, had carefully
explained the seriousness of their offence in terms that
Salazar had found surprisingly reasonable. Torriente
had then asked the boys, now that they could see
how the system worked, whether they had anything
to say for themselves. 'Seeing how something works
is different from being able to tell what it means,
and besides, asking us if we've got something to say
for ourselves is like offering a hanged man a last
request when you've already made up your mind to
hang him,' the Don had blurted with his customary
cheeky acumen.

Salazar was stunned. Not only had the Don not
said sorry but it had not even occurred to him to
do so. Never in a hundred years would Salazar have
responded in such a fashion, and yet the Don seemed
to have no idea how extraordinary it was for a boy
to speak in this way or, if he did, he could not have

thought there was anything unusual in being extraordinary. Nor did he seem to understand the way he came across to others, the depth of what he could grasp and say, and the manner in which others would view him because of it. He was, Salazar realised, neither as smug nor as aware as he seemed to be.

Learning from this weakness, Salazar gradually supplemented his own lack of raw talent with bluff, bluster and a keen eye for other people's faults, especially those of the Don. Much to his anger, however, the Don refused to acknowledge this metamorphosis and continued to treat Salazar as a giddy, but respectful, half-brother. This had continued to the point where even now, alone amongst all his acquaintances, the Don was the only person who considered Salazar to be a good and sympathetic listener.

Saluting a group of passing junior officers, Salazar pulled a Cohiba out of his pocket and, turning it in his mouth, lit it. The stumbling-block was that he would never repeat any of this to the Don's face. Once in the Don's company his resolve would fade, and a feeling of vast and infinite inferiority would drop through his being and out through his mouth. After all, anyone could become a two-star general, but there would only ever be one Don Rojo.

His driver opened the door for him and Salazar settled into the dark leather seat of his customised army-issue Mercedes. The night outside was unusually black with hardly a star visible in the sky. Salazar knew that if he strained his eyes he could make more appear but he did not care to. It felt like it was night all over the earth.

Once in his observatory Don Rojo, feeling the cold, changed into his 'wrecking' clothes. These were kept in a large trunk on top of a rusty set of lockers ordered from his old school. The clothes shared two unifying features: they were all too old to wear in society and none of them had actually been paid for. In this respect they were a testament to memory, as they were all gifts or acquisitions from comrades and old flames. The Don liked to hold these clothes up as lingering proof of his sentimentality, since, he liked to joke, there was little evidence of it anywhere else in his life. Although this was patently untrue it was exactly the sort of self-deprecation his friends allowed him to get away with, thus saving him from the embarrassment of admitting to his real faults.

Reaching up to the locker, he picked out a jacket that had been given to him by an Asturian miner, with whom he had fought back to back during the strike of '33. Standing in front of the mirror with it on provoked none of the feelings the Don had anticipated; rather than feeling bold or even ridiculous, he felt as if the jacket simply belonged to somebody else, to a younger and more confident man he had failed to remain true to.

The thought was a trite one, the difficulty with it being that the confident young man the jacket had once belonged to was, at the time, an anxious young man feigning confidence. A man for whom acting and essence were two parts of the same confusion. Unable to locate any core within himself that he was at ease with, the young Don had immersed himself in a hectic role-playing game that quickly established itself as the first premise of his essence. The result of this was that his personality seemed to come to him from somewhere else, from the people he copied openly and from those he admired secretly. Faultless as his ability to be other people was, the young Don still found himself troubled by a naive desire for authenticity. Since his essence was so clearly the result of his own hard work, it lacked the divine input that would make it, in the Don's eyes, completely genuine. Success helped to appease this internal quibble, but, in times of crisis, this sense of something missing was never far from the surface, its presence saturating his more immediate concerns. In fact, the Don reflected gloomily, when in a corner, his essence's dubious parentage could quite quickly collapse into a full-scale existential crisis. Such was the case now.

Blushing slightly, the Don shuddered as he remembered discussing this 'problem' far too frankly with Ernesto and Salazar earlier that week. Salazar, instead of reassuring the Don, as he normally did, by way of saying that the Don was the most authentic and grounded man he knew, had kept whatever he was thinking to himself. This was most unlike him. His years of acting had taught the Don a lot about other actors, and Salazar was most certainly another actor. Indeed, an actor who was at his most convincing when playing roles other than his own. This was why the Don knew something was afoot. And it wasn't just Salazar; other people's faces over the last few days were disguising things too. Women had avoided eye contact, close friends had been reluctant to talk, and he, whenever he became aware of these things, had felt as though he were going mad.

Things had not always been thus. The Don could still remember the tumultuous feeling of being cheered by thousands of peasants gathered outside his hacienda to celebrate the news of the land reform bill he had successfully passed. On that day they had clapped and clapped, it seemed as though they would never stop, and the Don had kept looking behind him to see whether there was someone else they were *really* clapping for. But the applause was all for him. Yet at the time he found the adulation easier to comprehend by pretending *not* to be who he was, just as he found the same tactic useful when dealing with intense pain. Who, he wondered, could bear to be themselves all the time without personas and fantasies to hide behind? It would, he decided, be like living in the nude.

All at once his body began to shake.

A car had pulled into his drive.

Antonio Mayle stepped out of the car and continued his journey to the house on foot. Carefully, he tied a scarf Lucille had given him around the scratches Muerta Astro had left on his neck. The light in the observatory scared him as the inference he drew from it was clear: he would now have to face Lucille *and* the Don. Lucille presented no more of a problem than any girl would in similar circumstances, but the Don was a big fish, often referred to but rarely known. If it came to a head-to-head between them it would be difficult to assess Antonio's chances, especially when playing away from home.

If he were able to confront the Don in daylight, however, facing a hand-picked audience of his own choosing, then, Antonio reasoned, the crown of one-upmanship might be his for the taking, but unfortunately the present conditions were unfavourable for the realisation of such a scenario. For one thing there was no crowd to play to, and for another, any clash would take place within the confines of four walls. Since much of Antonio's strength was derived from the ability to shout, interrupt and, ultimately, to appeal to the sky for inspiration, confined spaces, with their civilising tendencies, pushed him out of his depth.

Swearing mechanically, he lit a cigarette and eyed the front door with distaste. It was highly improbable that his slanderous opinions on the subject of the Don's mental health had not got back to him, just as it was improbable that he could keep avoiding the old man for ever. A meeting was inevitable, and, given that he had engineered the situation, the present moment would have to do.

Bolstered by this rare moment of courage, Antonio cleared his throat and, feeling his stomach sink, rang the doorbell.

An act he regretted before its completion.

Lucille led Antonio into the sitting room and parted the blinds that separated it from her old play area. 'You can sleep in here,' she said without emotion.

Antonio looked at the pile of old quilts stacked in neat heaps of three and clicked his tongue. 'Mmm, nice,' he murmured. 'But I think you'll need to explain this to me from the beginning.'

'I said you can sleep in here.'

'You're joking?'

'I am very tired and I don't want to argue with you tonight.'

'I'm sure that's true, but what I asked was whether you're serious . . .'

'*What*, you think that I don't really want you to sleep here?'

'I don't think you really want either of us to go to sleep at all.'

'Sleep here or go home, whichever.' With this Lucille turned on her heels and left the room.

A minute later she returned carrying a glass of water. 'Here, this is for you in case you get thirsty during the night.'

Antonio raised his eyebrows and licked his lips. For a second or two they both stared at each other. Lucille frowned and shook her head.

'You don't have any idea of how pathetic you are, do you?'

Antonio winked and pointed at his crotch.

Lucille snorted and left the room for a second time. Antonio bit his lip; he had expected the crotch movement to clinch it. Hesitantly, he shuffled to the door and watched Lucille ascend the staircase to her bedroom. At that moment what reality was, and what it felt like, were two separate things. Lucille wanted to be held tonight, if not by Antonio then by someone else. Anyone else. But her pride would not let her and now she was walking up the stairs alone, to lie down by herself. This was not what she wanted, but it was what was going to happen.

Antonio took off his coat, undid his laces and collapsed on to the quilts. He felt strangely relaxed and, if anything, relieved. The encounter with Lucille had been less savage than he deserved and the anticipated one with the Don had not even taken place. He had, it seemed, misjudged the situation.

Rather than entering the relationship game and stewing along the lines of 'How dare she!', Antonio turned his mind to the excuses he would invent to explain his lateness. In a few minutes Lucille would be tiptoeing down the stairs pining for him and, if she behaved, she might even be obliged. Adjusting his prick, he leaned back and grinned at the ceiling.

How good it was to feel so far ahead.

Chapter Eight

12.35 a.m. – the Tibidabo road

The car sped towards Nou Camp, its shiny black sides already thick with rain-sodden dust.

General Enrico Salazar-Rojo let out a deep breath and closed his eyes.

Sleep, which was usually an effortless activity for him to drop into, was tonight feeling like a long-distance run. This seemed to be the fault of his thoughts which, though banal, could not be accounted for within the terms of his habitual paranoia. The probable source of this mental disquiet was his memory which, since his conversation with Ernesto, had become fully activated.

Salazar opened one eye and then the other. Yawning loudly, he closed both, opened them, and then closed them again. If the price to be paid for falling asleep now was the loss of his memory and the experiences stored within it, then he would acquiesce gladly. That this mood should trail so closely behind that of his half-brother, the Don, was an irony that he would undoubtedly fail to appreciate.

His mood, provoked by half-remembered events that had occurred years earlier, had, since he stepped into the car, given way to an entirely unexpected avalanche of remorse which was slowly immersing Salazar in what felt like a world of shit. It was unfortunate for him that his sorrows, as well as his joys, had bled into his memory and that this memory, if dwelt on for long enough, contained the power to kill him. This was especially unfortunate since he did *not wish* to think about the past. A past marred by an overwhelming vagueness, developed through years of denial, that now prevented him from grasping the actual nature of his pain. All that was obvious was that the pain was there, that it had taken him by surprise, and that his memory's debris was entwined with the events of the past twelve hours.

Outside, refugees were moving to the side of the road to allow the car to pass. It would, Salazar reflected, be easy enough to give a few of the older ones a lift. Contemplation of his own power pleased him and a smile spread across his lips. This was the sort of thought he would have normally felt at home with, but because of Ernesto's bleating his head was still full of emotional dross. Few things repelled him more than having to pay attention to the contents of his mind in this way. It already seemed impossible to believe that only three hours earlier he had gamely fantasised about making love to his daughter-in-law, and five minutes before that considered the goal difference between Atlético and Real, and yet here he was driving himself mad like a first-year student of insanity. If he were to simplify his anxiety he would probably find that he was experiencing some form of belated guilt. Admittedly there was no one he felt any particular guilt about, and this realisation made him feel better. A guilt that was accountable to no one was the equivalent of a hideous poison introduced by a conscience too noble for its own good. With this thought firmly in the saddle, Salazar unwound the window and inhaled the cool night air.

A quarter of a mile farther up the road, Largo was preoccupied with guilt of a more immediate nature. Hot puffs of steam were rising like mist from the car bonnet and the engine was coughing and stuttering to a halt. At first he had tried to disguise this by fiddling with every gadget on the dashboard he could find, but now, as the bonnet of the car resembled nothing so much as a bonfire, he was forced to give up.

'I'm sorry but it looks like we're going to have to walk the rest of the way.' Largo winced.

The car had stopped dead.

'Are you in earnest, my tiny friend?' Josip asked with mock solemnity.

'I am, this car's had it, our immobility is the proof.'

For a minute everyone sat where they were and no one moved. The rain, beginning like a little finger flick but quickly breaking into a steady drum roll, had started again, and its sound echoed around the silent car.

'Okay, all of you, get out and give me a hand.'

Moving as though he were forsaking the comfort of a warm bath, the Captain stepped out of the car and, with the help of the other three men, turned it on its side.

Ali sighed. 'If we carry on on foot we won't get there until the morning.'

'So what do you think we should do?' Largo snapped back accusingly.

The Captain, ever aware of the responsibilities of being first in command, raised his hand and, realising that he had nothing to say, dropped it again quickly. Instinctively he found himself turning towards Josip, who was leaning against the upturned car.

'I think we'll have to hijack another vehicle,' Josip said matter-of-factly. 'Preferably one that works.'

'Look over there.' Largo pointed, relieved that the abuse he had anticipated had thus far failed to material-ise. Josip's eyes obeyed Largo's arm and stopped when they had reached the outline of Salazar's limousine, which was racing towards them dangerously.

Josip laughed. 'So we're saved.'

Antonio Mayle was beginning to get anxious. He had given Lucille ten minutes but there was still no sign of her. A woman's conception of time was not going to be the same as a clock's, but ten minutes was more than enough for her to realise she had made her point. He looked at his watch. Eleven minutes. He would give her twenty and then go home. Leaving without getting what he wanted was not a positive result, but nothing compared to staying on at the scene of his disappointment.

Antonio moved across the room and stood by the door. This whole experience made him wonder whether he could trust his romantic intuitions in the future, since his feelings for Lucille were qualitatively different from those he usually felt for girls. What was amazing was that she did not realise this or, more worryingly, realised it but didn't care. It was this fear that really stung Antonio, that it was possible for a woman to feel indifferent towards him in spite of, or perhaps because of, his declared interest in her. He had felt this particularly keenly when she had lost her temper and told him off. Her manner had been condescending and curiously uninvolved. The very fact that she had told him off was startling in and of itself, but the fact that he had let her do it at all meant something else – that he feared her. She scared him because he did not know how to respond to her, amuse her, or solve the problems she created, let alone understand them, and still come out on top. The unpalatable truth was that she stood on the other side of his limitations; that is, he knew he was not good enough for her.

Antonio stopped thinking and allowed this last thought to sink in. It was the first of its kind he had ever entertained, but now that it had occurred to him there was no going back. He would either survive it or demonstrate its truth.

He looked at his watch again.

Fifteen minutes.

The wallpaper in Rosa Rojo's room was the same colour as jam. When asked why this was so she would say that she owned a one-track mind. It pleased her that this reply was generally considered to be unintelligible, since it was her wish to be thought of as obscure. The puzzling aspect of this wish was its coexistence with a nature of remarkable simplicity. Disregarding a certain cynicism (it was natural for her to say 'bullshit' before 'I believe'), Rosa found it a struggle not to be ordinary. Neither her parents nor her sister were, but she was.

From the point of view of a report card, she was moderately good looking, fair at games, friendly to her friends, and she stored a large collection of scabs in a jar under her bed. Her perversity then was not so much a property of her essence as a feature of her reflexes. Her relationship with the world from this perspective was problematic, since any interaction with it increased the risk of making her cry. And this sat oddly with the rest of her personality. It was also, to her mind, the one special quality she possessed.

The family doctor had carefully explained that her fits of tears were only the most obvious symptom of acute sensitivity and a low pain threshold. But the Don, aware of his wife's disposition towards hysterics and its hereditary implications, remained sceptical and convinced that his daughter was nothing more than a sissy. 'It would be all right,' he said, 'if she restricted her tears to cuts and bruises, but this girl cries at the drop of a hat.' 'Don't be such a lummox,' her mother would say in her defence, 'girls will always cry when they're young. In a year or two she'll have grown out of it.' Unfortunately, her mother's optimism was unfounded, and by her nineteenth birthday Rosa was still capable of crying over a whole host of subjects ranging from the plight of orphans to bad skin. Surprisingly, none of this proved to have an adverse effect on her social life. If anything, the opposite was the case. The girls she knew, such as they were, viewed Rosa as a blessing in disguise. Things could have been so much worse, they reasoned. She could have been as beautiful as Lucille, her sister. As this was patently not the case, Rosa was adopted as their mascot; a harmless pet with a few charming eccentricities. The boys, keen to ingratiate themselves with her sister, did their best to take a protective interest in her, each as sure as the other that news of their heroism would find its way back to Lucille.

Pleased with all this attention and careful to give vent to her tantrums only in the presence of immediate family, Rosa began to cry less and enjoy herself more. Soon she was attracting followers of her own, difficult girls who were keen to emulate the Rosa Rojo path to social acceptance, and, of more interest to her, a number of earnest young men. These boys, perhaps lacking the confidence to chase more obvious beauties, settled for Rosa with the aim of consolidating a bohemian love affair. Without realising how, it occurred to Rosa that she had become a social force to be reckoned with, her immature affectations being confused for depth, and her lack of patience and narrowness of interests taken as the sign of single-minded genius.

For a while all went well. But in the end it was

only a matter of time before she overstretched herself (an abortive pass at the Captain during her sister's graduation reception being the first step along this path; true to form it ended in tears). Being a Rojo, Rosa had learned very little from this unfortunate experience and, people agreed, it would only be a matter of time before she would overstretch herself again.

Rosa sprang out of her bed feeling slightly startled. Though her room was pitch black and empty, something had obviously woken her, not a dream but something real and actual.

And then she heard it again. A muffled rapping on her door accompanied by a hoarse whisper: 'Please can you let me in, I'm not sure what I've done, I need to talk to someone.' Rosa leapt back into bed and pulled her sheets up over her ears and neck. She was utterly shameless in her fear.

'Please, we can help each other, just let me in and I'll explain,' hissed the voice at the door.

For a second Rosa believed that she was listening to the voice of a vampire. If she was, would certain rules apply? Primarily, the one forbidding a vampire to enter a room uninvited.

'Look, I'm coming in now. Please don't start shouting, I just want to chat.' And with this Antonio Mayle pushed open the door, turned on the main light, and walked up to Rosa's bed. Rosa blinked and groaned loudly, keen to pretend that the force of the light in her eyes was of greater importance to her than the fact that Antonio was only a few inches away from her face. One thing was for sure, though; she was no longer afraid.

He, for his part, was pleasantly surprised with what he now saw. Despite an uneventful face, Rosa's figure seemed to be more than just functional and, to his great satisfaction, it appeared that she was not the kind who wore any clothes in bed.

Throwing her unworn nightdress on to the floor, Antonio settled on to the stool next to Rosa's bed-head and offered her a cigarette.

Rosa was fully awake now, but there was nothing in Antonio's incredibly assured manner to suggest he found the situation he had created a strange one.

Rosa pushed the packet away from her face. 'I'm trying to give up,' she lied. She had been allergic to smoke since she was four.

'Me too.' He smiled, and lit a cigarette.

'Do you mind if I use this as an ashtray?'

Rosa glanced at the crystal vase he was pointing at and nodded, aware that if nothing else happened she had already experienced a moment to savour. A few seconds passed and the two of them sat in silence, Antonio smiling, with his legs stretched out in front of him, Rosa expressionless, her sheets tucked around her like a vast dress. At last she ventured, 'So, what have you done with my sister?'

'It's what she's done to me.'

'What do you mean?'

'She left me in your old playpen over an hour ago.'

'Why?'

'Not a word of explanation.' He shrugged. 'In fact I thought you would be able to tell me.'

'What makes you think I could do that?'

'Well, aren't sisters meant to know things about each other?' Antonio leered. 'And don't they help each other's boyfriends whenever they can?' he added.

'It depends on what sort of help you had in mind,' answered Rosa, and let her sheets slip down from her neck to the line of her breasts. Her own wantonness was coming as a pleasing shock to her.

Antonio's smile grew even broader. Rosa Rojo was an unexpected discovery. The type of sickly flirtation he was enjoying with her was just the sort of thing that made Lucille retch. And yet with Rosa there seemed to be a reciprocal rhythm emerging, a shared taste for the crass and obvious. Antonio stared at her closely. Maybe he was beginning to experience her as he willed her to be, but the outline of Rosa's face reminded him of Muerta's, as did her manner and presence in general. Or perhaps it was Muerta who reminded him of Rosa and he was confusing their respective importance, that in actual fact Muerta had been the dress rehearsal preparing him for Rosa, who would be the real feast. The speed of these thoughts, and their proximity to the shadow cast by Lucille, made Antonio recoil; he was forgetting about the job at hand.

'That painting up there,' he said, changing tack, 'did you do it?'

'Yes, it's one of mine,' stuttered Rosa, doing her best

to affect a husky purr, 'but you don't *do* paintings, you paint them.'

'Does it mean anything deep?' Antonio asked, moving up on to the bed and pressing his body against Rosa's.

'It's about the sea,' she intoned, glancing briefly at the painting of a large trout hung lopsided over her bed-head.

'And does it have a name?' said Antonio, pressing a hand under the first of her naked buttocks.

'Yes,' she breathed, 'it's called *The Tasty Fish*.'

Drawing his left arm around her neck to hold the length of her hair in a knot, he pulled her down. She met him with unexpected force, too much force, missing his mouth with the smear of her kisses, and bundling his fingers and thumb up into her damp cunt. Recoiling slightly, feeling robbed of his role as instigator, Antonio allowed Rosa to tug his trousers and pants down, suddenly aware that he was not ready for what was to come.

In less than a second Rosa knew too, freeing Antonio from her embrace to save him, momentarily at least, from further embarrassment. Wriggling on to his side, Antonio raised his head and tried to think of something to say. Looking at Rosa's naked body confirmed what he had feared; that if he failed to take her now he would never be able to consider himself a man again. Another second passed.

Rosa reached down and touched his prick. It was as limp as jelly. Still holding it, but bringing her head to his hand, she took his index finger and put it in her mouth. He felt its tip touch her throat. He was ready.

'You enjoyed that, didn't you?'

Antonio wiped the trail of come off Rosa's chest.

Rosa said nothing.

'What's the matter? Don't you feel like talking to me now?'

Antonio's manner was playful but matter-of-fact. Something had happened and he wanted to know what it was.

A gentle gust of air blew through the net curtains and travelled over Antonio's back, allowing him to feel cooler. It felt like an age since he had last made his mind up about something.

'I love it when that happens,' said Rosa, and she shut her eyes and breathed in deeply, letting her head rest beside Antonio's.

'You love it when what happens?'

'When the wind starts blowing around again, sending messages from place to place.'

Resisting the urge to make a joke about flatulence, and with genuine interest, Antonio asked, 'Is that happening now?'

Rosa put a finger to his lips and the two of them lay in silence.

After a while Antonio fell asleep.

'What did you shoot him for?' screamed Josip, his uniform covered liberally in the blood of a dead general.

'I don't know,' Ali replied. 'I'm sorry.'

Josip took the pistol out of his hand. Its handle was as cold as a dead man's hand.

'Well, ours is certainly turning out to be a century of violence.' Josip laughed, jocularly nudging Ali in the ribs. 'I mean, look who you've killed, for God's sake!'

'What in fuck do you expect me to tell them at Nou Camp?' cried the driver of the car, snapping out of his shock.

'Tell them your car was ambushed by fascists,' Josip answered flippantly, doing his best to remain jovial and in character.

'And what would I still be doing here alive if that happened?' screamed the driver of the ambushed car.

'Well, we can kill you as well if you like.'

The driver got out of the car and began running down the road.

'Come on, give me a hand with the body.'

Together Josip and Ali pulled General Salazar's corpse out of the car and dragged it across the water-logged road.

'We may as well leave it here. The fascists would hardly try to hide the thing.'

'What do you think the driver will do?' Ali asked uneasily.

'I'd say that by this time tomorrow he'll have defected to the fascists and will be claiming this kill as his own.'

Ali smiled slightly; the explanation settled his nerves.

'Not that you've got anything to be smug about,' Josip continued. 'Just because I haven't blown up in your face doesn't mean that I'm easy about this because, make no mistake, my friend, I'm not. To kill a general, even by mistake, is to fuck up big time.'

Josip paused to allow the words to have their required effect. Seeing that they had, he smiled and gave Ali a brotherly slap. It was good to take things, even big things, in your stride.

'Okay, let's get back to the car.'

Ali followed him obediently, now aware that, when confronted with reality, the hypothetical was quite rightly forgotten. Murder was no longer an ethical problem, but a practical one.

'Make way for the fastest gun in the West, the Sundance Kid.' Josip laughed.

'The Sundance Cunt,' snorted Largo.

'Perhaps you'll shut up and consider the consequences of this.' It was the first time the Captain had spoken since Ali had shot Salazar. Unlike the other three men he was slow to register a situation; as far as he was concerned, things had moved no farther than flagging the car down. Quickly, and deliberately, the Captain tried to take in what he saw.

Salazar's death, and Ali's reasons for killing him, were, he guessed, a reflex action typical of a boy showing off. Either way they were not things he cared to look too deeply at. For if he was to keep up with the action it would pay to stay close to the surface.

'So what, now that we've shut up, *are* the consequences of this fuck-up?' asked Josip, trying not to smile.

'The consequences . . .' said the Captain as slowly as he could. 'The consequences are . . .'

Josip started to laugh; he had long grown used to the Captain's belief that he was expected to provide an answer to everything, even things that he did not have an answer to.

'What will happen now,' the Captain continued, his mind back on track again, 'is that we carry on moving as quickly as we can.'

'I thought that's what we'd be doing anyway,' spluttered Largo cautiously, nervous whenever he was sure he was right about something.

Ali, however, had seen the same loophole as the Captain, and unlike his superior wished to take advantage of it. 'I don't understand. I mean, if this man's dead' – Ali pointed over to Salazar's body, which, to Largo's eyes at least, still appeared to be moving – 'if he's dead then what's to stop us calling this off? They were his orders, weren't they? He's the one that wants the Don dead, isn't he?'

'Are you trying to tell me that you think by murdering one man you can get out of killing another?' the Captain replied angrily, cross that everything he said now appeared open to amendment. 'Besides, there's a lot you don't understand about the military. For one, there's such a thing as a chain of command, orders don't start and stop with just one person. Also, an order isn't the same thing as a whim or enthusiasm that happens just because someone in power wants it to, they're made for reasons. Reasons that you may be ignorant of for your own safety.'

'Come on, now,' Josip interjected, 'don't get so carried away. I don't think he's as far off the mark as you're suggesting, and anyway, don't tell me that you weren't thinking exactly the same thing. Your speech about military matters is true as far as it goes but in war people can try things on, and get away with a lot too.'

'I thought you'd at least have some idea of what you're talking about, Josip.'

'I have. Salazar organised this ride and you, and then we, agreed to go on it – on that we all agree. We're here, then, because of his orders, but if he's dead then so are they. So what's the point of seeing this through? Pleasure?'

'Josip' – the Captain's expression was pained but not impatient – 'do you mind me asking you a question?'

Josip grinned and prepared himself for a speech.

'Why do you think we're out here tonight?'

'To send Don Rojo into the next life.'

'No, that isn't what I meant. *Why* do we have to do it?'

'Because those were the orders that dead bastard Salazar gave us.'

'Yes, but why were we going to carry them out, *what was in it for us*?'

Josip's face hardened noticeably. 'In it for us? Fifteen

thousand pesetas each or exemption from service at the front, if I remember rightly.'

'And you think it was in Salazar's power to grant us all that? Was it hell! He may have wanted the Don out of the picture but you can bet the orders came from farther up . . .'

'From who, then?'

'The Russians maybe, I don't know, who cares anyway, the point is that if the orders didn't come from Salazar neither will the reward nor the punishment for failing to carry them out.'

Josip spat into the road. 'I'm not scared of being sent to the front . . . but I could still use the money. I hadn't thought about it like that, though, killing him just for the money, I mean.'

Ali, who had no need of the money and positively longed to be sent to the front, nodded and added in as gruff a voice as he could, 'Yeah, but we could all use the extra bucks.'

'But we've got to go through with it now anyway, haven't we?'

All three men turned to Largo.

Smiling lecherously, he pointed to Salazar's corpse, which, at last, seemed to have stopped moving.

'If we hadn't, I mean if Ali hadn't, killed the general, how would we know he was dead, that his orders were no longer valid . . . ?'

'We could have been the first to find his body,' Ali volunteered hastily, unsure as to how this observation fitted in with what they had been talking about.

'We aren't even meant to be here, let alone rocking into Nou Camp with a bullshit story like that. The sequence of events would be as follows. First they'd claim they didn't know who we were. Then they'd shoot us.'

'You're wrong, our own people wouldn't do that to us.'

'No, I'm not. If our people wouldn't kill us they'd get some of those Russians to. Believe me, that lot wouldn't attach any more significance to our lives than they would a stroll in the park or a week of hot weather.'

'So, what would you have us do, then?'

'All I'm saying is that news can travel fast. If we bump the Don off in the next half-hour, this guy's death becomes the stuff of explicable phenomena.'

'Exactly,' said the Captain. 'Rather than having to keep our heads down and hope that no one asks us about a dead general whose orders we failed to carry out, we kill the Don and this will look like an immediate retaliation – one of theirs for one of ours, as the dead general over there would have it,' and he pointed at Salazar's body, which had started to twitch again.

'I'm sorry but I don't understand.'

'Understand what, Josip?'

'That both these men, Salazar and the Don, are *ours,* they're Republicans, and the fascists know they are, so what sense would there be in anyone retaliating against their own side?'

'But that's the point, only one of them *was* on our side, and that's the one that's already dead.'

'I'm sorry?'

'It's what I meant in the first place. Why do you think we were really asked to kill Don Rojo?'

Slowly Josip's squint settled into an uncomfortable smile.

Largo laughed out aloud. 'I think he understands.'

12.50 a.m. – the Perez-Baroba fair

'Who else knows he was going to defect?' Alcazar's face seemed to have lost weight, excitement and curiosity making him hungry.

'The Russians and the people Salazar's sent out to kill him.' Ernesto Rojo paused and stared around the field uncomfortably, before adding, 'At the very least.'

'Well, I wonder who else he would have broadcast it to. What about the fascists themselves . . .'

'I don't know, Braulio is unpredictable like that. He felt open enough about his position to talk to Salazar – which is something I'd never have done no matter how strong my doubts were – but, as far as I know, he's had no official contact with the enemy.'

Alcazar shook his head. 'So how serious can he be about defecting if he hasn't told the enemy of his plans but, and this is what I can't believe, *has* told an officer on our own, and very paranoid, general staff.' Alcazar took his cap off and brushed the water off the top of it.

'He's one of the biggest idiots I've ever come across,' he growled disbelievingly.

'But he has deeply complicated reasons for being like that,' Ernesto joked feebly.

Alcazar snorted and picked up a handful of empty magazine cartridges. Being in a position to help someone he had once been friends with was a rare occurrence. And yet . . .

'I admire your loyalty, Ernesto, but if what you said is true, I can't see how I can help your brother now.'

'But you can, Raul. This *paseo* hasn't, as far as I know, been sanctioned at the highest level yet. Salazar was only nudged into ordering it tonight on the flimsiest of pretexts, ones that I think he helped make up in the first place. I doubt whether anyone higher up even knows what is going on.'

'I thought you said the Russians did.'

'You know what they're like, all you've got to do is mention a name and they'll okay murder.'

'So if you're not even sure that Braulio's going to defect then what other motivation does Salazar have for ordering his murder?'

'He told me that no one's above our laws. Here are the Russians giving us all this help and there's Braulio whingeing like a spoilt bastard about our loss of autonomy and how the fascists aren't really such bad chaps after all. Or, if you prefer, the anarchists have been out of control – popping anybody who owned a few acres before the war. Well, Salazar arrested a few and now wants to show what a consistent man of iron he is by having Braulio taken out on trumped-up treason charges.'

'Come on, Ernesto. What's his real motive?'

'Quite probably personal things that stretch right back to when we were all children . . .'

'Are you meaning to tell me . . .'

'I'm serious. His reasons may be perverse but for him they're real enough.'

'Supposing I accept that, and I'm prepared to because I know the type of reactive dog Salazar is, well, even then we're still compromised by the question of your brother's loyalty. Because it doesn't matter what Salazar's reasons for wanting him dead are – if Braulio's going over to the fascists he's a dead man anyway.'

Ernesto rubbed a trail of sweat into his hairline and bit his lip. He was, all of a sudden, very conscious of his overall appearance. His high forehead and narrow eyes, the double chin and shapeless arse, but most of all the general lack of identification with his own body.

'Are you all right, Ernesto?' Alcazar laid his hand on the smaller man's shoulder.

'Yes . . . I'm fine. But I'm not sure how to answer your question because I'm not sure of the answer.'

The pain in his chest was too great to be true. All that could follow a sensation as intense as this was death, and Enrico Salazar knew it. Slowly he began to drag his cut and bleeding body over the Tibidabo Road, repeating the same mantra: 'Be active, don't think, be active, don't think, be active . . .'

Before the car had left, it had run over both his legs, crushing them completely. He was unconscious when this happened, but its effects were all too clear to him now. He had been proud of his legs, but they were of much less concern to him than the hole in his chest made by the bullet.

'Oh Jesus Christ help me,' he whispered.

The line of Ernesto's pencil-thin moustache was saturated in perspiration.

'I don't think that at the moment Braulio knows his own mind.'

'You mean he's going mad?'

'No, nothing as simple as that.' Ernesto Rojo shivered and folded his arms. Alcazar beckoned to an orderly, who offered Ernesto a large trench-coat which he accepted at once.

'If not that, then what?'

Ernesto took a deep breath. 'I believe that at least one-third of Braulio's brain is informed by something even he doesn't know the nature of. But whatever it is, it's not madness.'

'This is becoming too subtle for me.'

'I'm sorry, I'll try and put it more crudely. I think there have been some major shifts in Braulio's thinking that he's had trouble keeping up with.' Ernesto drew his hand up to the side of his face, covering it as he spoke. He felt pathetic. Firstly for having to ask for something that he was too weak to cope with by himself, but also for skirting around the obvious so ineptly. For if God writes stories for each of us that we are compelled to follow, then the Don had lost the plot of his. This was so obvious that Ernesto realised that he had already made things more complicated than they were.

'Go on . . .'

'Well . . . Braulio has started to become quite disenchanted with the Republic,' Ernesto began unconvincingly. A strong wind was blowing across the field and he could feel his voice becoming lost in it.

'For what sort of reasons?'

'Oh, you know, usual ones.'

'No, I don't.'

Ernesto hesitated. For some reason he had expected Alcazar to be more understanding.

'The Republic pays me and I'm satisfied with my pay, so how would I know what his reasons are?' pressed Alcazar.

'They're definitely more run of the mill than ideological.'

'So they're just pragmatic, then?'

'Yes, I think that's what they are really.'

'So could I trouble you for a few examples?'

'You could, but I think they'd sound very petty and, in a way, I think it's menial things that have caused them. Things like the bureaucracy . . . the slowness with which everything moves. Braulio . . . lacks patience with the imperfection of everyday life, and I think he expects much more from it than it can provide.'

'That makes him a spoilt bastard but not a defector.'

'I know that . . .'

'Just give me something to get my teeth into.'

'I'm trying! I just don't know what to tell you. My brother's . . . I've no better idea of what goes on in Braulio's head than . . .'

'Ernesto, I've got a better idea. Just give me some facts, something which might explain why other people might think he'd want to defect. Why someone like Salazar or the Russians would think he'd want to defect.'

'All right, the facts . . . Two days ago Braulio asked for a meeting with Salazar, and Salazar asked me to come along. Braulio turned up, you could see that he had been drinking, and went straight into a tangent. You know, a real epic like the ones he used to give in college. It lasted for about ten or fifteen minutes and covered everything; tradition, love of country, El Cid, acting – you get the picture. The difference was there was a real patriotic edge to all this, quite a bit of talk about uniting the two Spains and some pompous stuff towards the end about national salvation. I think he knew he wasn't carrying us with him, though, because when he wound up, he asked us if we felt the same way too.'

'And what did you tell him?'

'I told him that I didn't know what he was talking about, of course.'

'And what did Salazar tell him?'

'Salazar, now I come to think of it, didn't say anything, which is a bad sign in itself.'

'But the Don didn't actually say anything about defecting, then?'

'Not exactly, but he did say that he had changed his mind about the national question, and Salazar understood this to be a coded way of saying that he intended to defect.'

'I'm not at all sure that I would have come to the same conclusion.'

Ernesto shook his head sullenly. 'God knows what he really means. I know that I'm tired of having to think about it.'

Alcazar passed his old friend a crushed packet of cigarettes.

'Here, help yourself.'

'No thanks.'

'Suit yourself,' said Alcazar, and took one out of the pack for himself, pleased that he had successfully restricted his smoking to night-times. 'For what it's worth I'm going to tell you what I think. And don't worry, it isn't going to be too bad. You see, I think you were there earlier with that amateur psychology you were employing.'

'What, about the Republic?'

'No, about your brother's brain. I've known him nearly as long as you and the stuff about his brain seems intuitively sound to me.'

'How exactly?'

'Two-thirds of his brain is really wide of the mark, so

he forgets to employ caution when roaming around in this other third, the part he doesn't know about. He's such a pompous bastard that he refuses to see that even if *he's* investigating this third in the spirit of impartial enquiry, there are others out there itching to nominate him fascist of the month.'

'So you don't think he's serious about defecting?'

'No, of course not. He's just had a bad day at the Cortes and has been reading too much Cervantes. In a week he'll be Pancho Villa again.'

'So you'll help me?'

Alcazar smiled. 'Of course I will.'

Salazar had stopped his mantra once his throat had begun to hurt as much as his stomach. His thoughts had briefly turned to his legs again and how well they tanned in the sun. It was then that the verge of the Tibidabo Road seemed farther away than ever, and something he had never expected to happen did; he died.

Chapter Nine

1.15 a.m. – the Tibidabo road

Lucille held the bicycle clip to her arm, and less than a mile away the Captain repeated the same movement. The movement of their arms was accompanied by another in their hearts. For Lucille the regularity of this affliction helped steady its pain. She sat on her bed unmoved, her patrician composure intact. The same was not true of the Captain. The pain, and its recollective effect on his memory, seemed to break the night up into disparate and quarrelling elements. Slowly, he sought to separate those memories that were worth salvaging from those that could only hurt. Gradually his mind settled on an image of dubious authenticity. The scene he visualised had a heavy air of the idyllic running through it, and he disliked the way his memory attributed this quality to almost every experience it processed. As such it prevented him from ever grasping the direct completeness of an event, his memory always ready to wrap it in the fine embroidery of a fable. Nevertheless, this particular image seemed stronger than any objection levelled against it. He could see himself and Lucille walking across a harvested field during an autumn some years earlier. In front of them was a sunset he could not keep his eyes from, as if he expected it to show him something. It failed to; autumn had finished, and with that came the onset of winter thoughts.

The night once again felt fragmented.

'I refuse to believe that he was the smartest person in your year. He couldn't even get the better of Marcus Pardoe,' Ali was protesting.

'That's because he didn't think Pardoe was worth bothering with,' Largo replied quickly.

'Smart isn't the same as sly. He's a sly cunt and that's all he was.'

'And a coward and a fucking draft-dodger,' added Josip with grim emphasis.

'You chumps would say that now you're conscripted. I'm just giving credit where it's due. I agree that he's a good-for-nothing but, in the end, Antonio Mayle gets the last laugh and all the best pussy,' Largo declared finally.

'Even if you're right, which you're not, that still wouldn't make him the smartest person to come through St Juan's,' protested Ali.

'You sound jealous of the man's achievements.'

'I can't believe I'm hearing you say this,' interrupted the Captain, who belatedly realised that he had a stake in this argument. 'If it was left to Mayle you'd be nailed to a clipboard in a damned freak show.'

The quarrel in the car had re-established the supremacy of the real over the remembered, reminding the Captain, paradoxically, that he was still angry at having had to explain details of the Don's defection. What was especially annoying about this was that he was not sure he had needed to, but he had felt forced to, just to reassert his authority. Salazar had even said that the information was top secret. The Captain paused. Not far away from him, in fact much closer than he would like, he could feel the familiar stirrings of oncoming panic. Acting quickly, he began to reason it out of his system. His conversation with Salazar had taken place a full day ago – now Salazar was dead and they were riding in his car to the Don's house. The panic seemed justified, but alternatively, seen from another point of view, he knew he was capable of reducing it to nothing. In circumstances like these it was best to stop thinking and just ride one's luck. A close analysis of the situation could wait until the memoirs.

'Does someone have to do you a good turn for you to hate them, Largo?' Josip laughed.

'You reward your friends by talking down to them because you can't understand why a loser like you has friends,' interjected Ali keenly, already unsure whether this was really a speech worth making, but aware that it was preferable to sitting in silence. 'Perhaps if we treated you like what you believe you are, you'd run and tell Antonio how much you respect us as men and studs.'

'Look, that isn't what I . . .'

'You know, Largo, I don't think any of us care too much for your point here,' interrupted the Captain.

'For . . .'

'Enough, we've heard enough.'

'You're all arrogant,' Largo whispered, 'an arrogant deluded bunch of . . .'

Josip and Ali started to laugh but the Captain, with the customary aristocratic disdain befitting one who never thought he was wrong, had already stopped listening.

It was no secret that he and Antonio Mayle hated each other's guts. Of the two, Antonio tended to voice his hatred more loudly, but no one doubted the silent contempt in which the Captain held him. It was a big mistake to tell either of them that they were alike (as Lucille had once, and now regretted), or even mention one's name to the other in any context other than that of abuse. Though it was generally agreed that Antonio had been the more successful of the schoolboy rivals, it was acknowledged that he lacked, and would always lack, the Captain's class, though quite what this class was remained the subject of some controversy.

So why, thought the Captain, is Lucille sleeping with him now? It was not a thought he usually wished to tackle directly for obvious reasons. Nevertheless the night had been a great shedder of inhibitions, even mental ones. Perhaps it was time to consider the hitherto inconsiderable, that Antonio, in spite of whatever had happened in the past, was now Lucille's first choice.

'Could you open the window, Largo?'

'You've already got yours open.'

'I know, but I want yours open so we can get some circulation going in here.'

'Don't argue with him, Largo, it's physics,' mumbled Josip sullenly.

Again the Captain tried to impose order on his thoughts and extract a moral from them. What did they say about the type of love he felt for Lucille? That it was impossible for him to have envisaged a practical future with her, or that life would have had to have felt real first for love to have?

'Largo.'

'Yes, Captain?'

'I'm sorry for sounding like I'm snapping at you, it's not serious enough to . . .'

'I know.' Largo smiled, reaching back with one arm and tapping the Captain lightly on the head. 'And I'm sorry for even responding,' he added slightly portentously.

The Captain grinned indulgently and bit his tongue. Largo could have the last word.

'The stupid thing is that I don't even give a shit about that dung-eater Mayle anyway,' continued Largo fair-mindedly. 'I hate guys like him who always leave a situation thinking they're in the right.'

The Captain said nothing, even though he could already hear what he wished to add tugging at his tongue. He knew, though, that what remained unsaid was the impression he wanted to make and not what he needed to say.

'Yeah, you've read that guy correctly,' Largo added by way of a conclusion.

The Captain had not always 'read that guy correctly',

but his failure to had already become a lesson well learnt. Not that his present attitude to Antonio was any less embarrassing. He despised the shameful but necessary jealousy he felt towards him, finding its force impossible to resist. To think that Lucille, who existed exclusively for him, at the centre of his orbit, for whom there was little he did not feel with or for, now held the same position for Antonio was more than he could bear. Though the years had changed his opinion of many of her qualities, he remained devoted to the person they belonged to. This, and knowing it was his fault that she and Antonio had met in the first place, led the Captain to the most painful of conclusions. That he had been a stopgap in Lucille's destiny, and not its realisation.

'Brooaghh,' Largo gargled. 'It's been a long time since I've driven one of these things.'

It had been. Not since Don Rojo had allowed the crippled son of their deranged cobbler to sit on his father's lap and steer their limousine had Largo ridden in a car like this.

'I'm glad you're finding the experience so rewarding,' the Captain intoned neutrally.

'Yeah, and I'll tell you something else. It's not often you hear Josip singing so well.' Largo signalled towards the back seat.

'Or hear him singing this song,' added Ali.

'Or singing at all,' finished the Captain, dryly aware of his position as last on the chorus line.

Josip, whose singing voice, like his speaking one,

was distinctly regional, continued to sing, as he stared absent-mindedly into the passing countryside. The song, usually sung unaccompanied by a woman, belonged to his parents' generation. When Josip first heard it he had yet to experience the emotions contained in its words, but the power of the singer's expression had convinced him of their truth. Now he felt that the song had anticipated the most important experiences of his life, and that these experiences had grown even more powerful and complete with each rendition.

It was a song about which the Captain had mixed feelings. There were other songs of the same period he could still listen to, but this was not one of those. This song could only ever remind him of a single person. And less than half a mile away she began to cry.

1.35 a.m. – an unnamed track nine kilometres north of the Rojo hacienda

'What I'm saying is that no amount of insights into the world are worth shit if they hamper your operational ability,' bellowed Alcazar from the turret of the commandeered half-track. Ernesto, squatting directly beneath him, nodded vigorously. He was only half listening.

'That's why I love a wartime army. It's paradise. As soon as you have an idea you act on it.'

Ernesto Rojo had failed his army medical on account of being flat footed, but tonight he could see things from Alcazar's point of view. Speeding through the countryside on the back of a half-track was proving to be an invigorating experience.

'Fork left at the junction,' yelled Alcazar. 'At this rate we'll be at the Don's in less than twenty minutes.'

Disappearing into the turret and appearing a minute later with a bottle of brandy, Alcazar clutched Ernesto's arm. 'Here, have a swig of this.'

Ernesto drank deeply and returned the bottle to Alcazar. 'After all these years it's great to see that the bonding process still has its own momentum.'

'It won't be finished until we've both been swept off the face of this earth,' roared back Alcazar, taking his second heavy swig.

'Or until our stuffed heads decorate the . . .'

'Jesus, the fucking path's mined!'

The half-track ahead of them was in flames and burning men were running in every direction.

'It's not a mine. Someone's dropping bombs on us.'

'Over there, he's running towards those farmhouses.'

'Nobody shoot. Take him alive.'

So this, thought Ernesto, is combat. Rather like normality with dangerous things happening in it. It seemed almost ordinary; people either falling over or looking like they had just lost something.

Alcazar was tugging at his arm and gesturing at the ground wildly. Ernesto obeyed the movement. The whole experience was taking on the strangest of associations, and he found himself recalling the attitude to fear he had formed at school. Fear never happened in the way he expected it to, that is, with the arrival of some larger-than-life giant, but always within the same mundane reality he normally inhabited. The figure that scared him could just as well have been a giant, but in fact remained as small as it was before it had begun to scare him. That this could happen was the cause of real fear. Perhaps he would ground-test the theory later with Alcazar over a beer.

'I thought I told you to get down and to keep down.' A grenade exploded, scattering its load over the road, and Ernesto's fear became slightly less theoretical. Combat was not the same as being intimidated by pretty girls at school. Similar in theory, but much worse in degree.

'For God's sake, get your arse level with your head!'

Ernesto complied.

'Now stay put, I'm going forward.' Alcazar bounded across the road, over the flooded ditch, and into the darkness of a nearby field.

Ernesto watched him go with interest. Even here, his greatest fear belonged not to the moment but to his mind, the fear of not being able to understand something, greater even than his desire for self-preservation.

The firing continued for what might have been a few moments; Ernesto had no way of telling for sure, his concentration focused on nothing beyond the patch of earth his nose was pressed against.

'Here, Dr Rojo. Here's our man.'

Ernesto leaned back and peered over his shoulder. Crouched behind him were two of Alcazar's men, and squashed between them, on all fours, a civil guard. The bones in his face, and those in his hands, had been completely smashed.

'His face and hands are smashed up.'

'I know, Doctor, but it still doesn't stop his breath from stinking like a distillery.'

It was true, the man reeked of alcohol.

'We thought you would want to question him.'

The shooting had definitely stopped now and Ernesto got up.

'Yes, you were right to think that, Sergeant.' *I'm in charge here*, thought Ernesto, *I'm really in charge here.* This was his flash-point, his limit experience, either to take charge of the men in the field, or to fail to.

'How many of you are there?' he heard his voice say.

The man looked up. He was broken. Now all he wanted to do was live.

'Eight or nine,' the man croaked through his broken jaw.

'What were you doing on that hill before you decided to attack us?' Ernesto pointed up at the burning church in the distance. 'You Nationalists are supposed to believe in God, for Christ's sake,' he added in his best soldierly fashion.

The man pressed the palms of his hands against his face to stem a tide of blood.

'It was horrible . . . I don't remember anything, I swear to you I don't, I was too drunk, I can't remember a thing.'

'They're probably the tail-end of that rabble we dealt with earlier at the fair, they're the same mish-mash. This cunt isn't even a civil guard. Look at his trousers.' The sergeant stabbed the end of his bayonet into the man's leg as if to emphasise the point.

'That's enough, Sergeant,' barked Ernesto, amazed at, and enjoying, his new-found ability to determine reality with his voice.

Holding the unfortunate prisoner's chin in his hand, Ernesto stared down into his eyes with a macho solemnity worthy of Alcazar himself. 'Now listen to me, you mean little bastard. You look to be at quite a disadvantage now, but I'm willing to bet that's not the way you looked to those people on the hill whose homes you've just turned to firewood. Now I don't know who you are, or what possessed you to come behind our lines, but I'm willing to bet that you do, and if you don't tell me now I'll kill you myself.'

The man burst into tears and began stuttering indecipherably.

I've done that to him, thought Ernesto, *I've just done that to him.*

'Come on, now, what are you saying? Speak clearly.'

'The others, at the fair, they were the diversion,' the man muttered quickly.

'What, a diversion for you?'

'No, not for us, we're a diversion too.'

'A diversion for what, then?'

'For the assassins.'

*   *   *

Antonio Mayle breathed out contentedly and buried his head farther into Rosa Rojo's chest. It was the most peaceful moment of his life. Beneath him Rosa twitched silently and stared out of her window. The sense of achievement she had felt an hour earlier had been replaced by another, less familiar but more engrossing emotion, that of being released from herself. For the first time in her life she felt like air. She wanted to tell someone about it but there was no point. What was there to say about the complete absence of feeling that she was experiencing at this, most pivotal, point of her life? Drawing away from Antonio, she turned to the wall and closed her eyes.

'What assassins?' The man's face was bleeding again. 'What assassins are you talking about?' Ernesto's elation was fast turning into impatience.

'There are two of them with a list. We were told to go and make fireworks while they did their dry operation.'

'Stop there. I want you to explain this from the beginning. This list, what is it?'

'The addresses of your top people. They want to fuck with your chain of command.'

'And you're meant to be here keeping us busy?'

The man nodded.

'Sir, you know I recognise this man. We were in reform school together. He must have been released from prison for this night trip.'

The man nodded again. 'Some of us were, but not

all of us. Not me. I was released in the amnesty after the election . . .'

'Do I look like I care?' interrupted Ernesto. 'What I want to know is who's on this list, this death-list of yours?'

The man sped through a sequence of names, some of them familiar, others less so. Ernesto's blood didn't freeze until he heard the name of his brother.

'You said Don Rojo.'

The man paled. 'Did I?'

The guard brought his rifle down on the man's back. 'You know you fucking did.'

'You said Don Rojo,' Ernesto repeated. 'You said Don Rojo. Have they already killed him, have they already killed Don Rojo?'

'No, they wouldn't have yet, there's no way they would have – he's the biggest name on the list. He'll be last.'

'Why? I don't understand.'

'Because once he's shot, the alarms'll go off. Then they wouldn't have the chance to kill anyone else.'

'Sergeant, shoot him.'

A shot rang out, folding the man in half like a deckchair.

Ernesto wiped a handful of blood off his face.

'How many of the half-tracks are still working?'

'The first two and the one at the back.'

'Right, let's collect your colonel and move out of here at the double.'

*   *   *

Alcazar was on the verge of the hill beckoning to the others on the road below. Ernesto, leaving the half-tracks guarded, made his way up with the rest of the men.

The first thing that struck him was the air. It reminded him of the smell of a dead animal killed crossing the road on a wet day. Alcazar was standing next to a well in the forecourt area of the surrounding houses. In the semicircle formed by him and his men stood a naked woman in her sixties and a small boy.

The old lady pointed to a body lying a few yards away. 'That's my son. The one next to him is his friend, David.'

The second boy had been blindfolded and, judging by the network of fresh injuries covering his back and chest, clubbed to death. Alcazar rolled the body of the old woman's son on to its front. The stomach had been cut open and the eyes dug out.

'My boy was in the army for two years. My husband, his father, was also a soldier. They both . . .' The woman's voice trailed off into a sound that predated language. Ernesto held his hands over his ears. Ignoring the woman, Alcazar walked over and offered him a cigarette. Ernesto accepted.

'I hate recapturing a place. That's when it's always the worst, when you recapture a place,' Alcazar said emotionlessly.

Ernesto found himself nodding in agreement. Slowly the scene sank in. A score of bodies lay scattered in various places, some animal, some human, each one

emerging and growing, as it were, from the camou-
flage crafted by the wrecked settlement. Alcazar sat
down on the well's ledge and picked up the little
boy.

'You've been a brave little man,' he said, rubbing the
boy's ears and neck.

The boy smiled faintly and replied, 'Are you proper
soldiers?'

Alcazar nodded.

'They said we were in wireless contact with you,' the
boy continued.

'Did they?' said Alcazar. 'Have you ever seen a
wireless before?'

'I don't know,' the boy answered.

'Sir.'

'What?'

'We've found the boy's brother.'

'Where?'

'Nailed to the barn door.'

'And the rest of the family?'

'There was another kid alive in the cow stall. We're
sending him back to the half-track with the old lady.'

'Any others?'

'Yes . . . In the chapel.'

The front of the chapel had been gutted by flames
and a pair of burnt skeletons, their hands still chained
together, lay trapped in the smouldering debris. Behind
them, on the altar, lay a young girl naked except for her
shoes and socks. She had been shot in both hands, and
the lower half of her body resembled nothing so much

as a crumbling brick. She was still alive. Next to her lay another girl, in a similar state but shot in the chest and face. She was dead.

'I've had enough,' said Ernesto.

There was nothing else to say.

Down by the half-track, Ernesto finished his second cigarette of the evening and the second of his life.

'I thought all this was just propaganda,' he heard a voice say.

'The propaganda people have to get their ideas from somewhere.'

'Don't worry, we'll give their propaganda people plenty to work with too.'

Three survivors of the raiding party that had attacked the village were captured by Alcazar's men; another found drunk in the barn. The first two were tied to the half-tracks and torn in half, a third spared for questioning, the drunk hacked to pieces where he lay.

Alcazar helped Ernesto back up on to the half-track.

'It's time we found your brother and told him he's made some evil enemies.'

Ernesto nodded in silent agreement before mumbling incoherently, 'Men and guns, that's what we look to. *That's* what saves us.'

Alcazar smiled deprecatingly and shook his head. 'No, the fact that each moment is followed by the next moment, *that's* what saves us.'

2 a.m. – Don Rojo's observatory

Don Rojo rubbed his eyes and hauled himself up off the observatory floor. Now was no time to consider, or be fearful of, the personas he had gathered during his life. Certainly, the fact that he had, over the past few months, been feeling increasingly removed from himself was a matter of concern to him, but it was a matter better dealt with in the warmth of his own bed. Besides, discomfort was only worthwhile when it proved a point, and as his doze on the observatory floor had been unobserved it therefore proved nothing. Taking off the Asturian miner's jacket, so that he was naked again, the Don made his way back down the spiral staircase to his bedroom.

It was difficult to pick out the moment when he had first felt, and then allowed, things to slide. The warning signs were experienced in practical ways, of this the Don could be sure. The time, for example, was never what he thought it was, and whenever he looked at a clock he found he was always an hour or so out. This realisation, which in itself was both trivial and obvious, hit him with the force of a thousand associated horrors, each derived from, and related with in ways that only he could see, his inability to keep time correctly. Noises too, even the most harmless of them, had started to sound as if they were specifically addressed at him, developing to the point where even the rumble of the plumbing sounded like the sighs of his wife making love to someone else. Gradually he had come to systematise this paranoia, but his move towards rationalisation legitimated it, and allowed it to become the full-blown madness he now feared he was on the verge of. Worse still was the way in which it felt less like madness and more like the truth, a truth that only habit and boredom had concealed in the past. The conclusion was ugly; he would never be able to trust *reality* in the same way again.

There was, of course, still a part of him that resisted this verdict; that believed he had given the voices in his head too much autonomy and forgotten that it was his right to disagree with them if he wished to. But he had no more reason to trust this verdict than the other, less reassuring one, and if assurance was what the Don was after he was least likely to find it now that he needed it the most.

He would just have to act.

There were muffled sobs coming from Lucille's room. Opening her door, he found her lying face down on the floor. For some reason he expected her to be covered in bruises, but on picking her up he found that there were none.

'He hasn't beaten you up?' he asked. There was no response from Lucille so, changing tack, he held her up in a bear hug and gently rubbed his nose into the nape of her neck. Softly, he whispered, 'There, now, what's the matter with you, then?'

'Just go away and leave me alone.'

The Don ignored the remark and held her more tightly.

'I asked you to leave me alone,' Lucille insisted.

The Don held more tightly still and repeated his question.

'Just leave me alone, will you!' Lucille brought her knee up against her father's groin, causing him to drop to the floor in a mixture of agony and embarrassment.

All of a sudden he was very aware of his nakedness.

'What did I do to deserve that?'

'Please, could you please just leave me alone, you fucking fool!'

Lucille had never sworn at the Don before, but if he felt any sense of slight he did not show it as he crawled back out of her room on all fours.

The goatherd moved over Salazar's dead body methodically. He had not held out much hope of finding a great deal, and he had not been proved wrong. Within minutes his work was finished. With him he took a wedding ring and a photo of Muerta Astro found in Salazar's inside pocket. As he had no interest in football the goatherd had thrown the tickets for the Real game over the hedge. Between them, forever to be suspended in speculative uncertainty, lay the uncountersigned order for Don Rojo's assassination.

So now the Don knew. Madness was made true through recognising it for what it was. The complexity he had attributed to it was true but only to a point, for madness knew how to be simple too. It was when no one laughed at your jokes, considered you interesting, or wanted your love.

It was when your daughter kneed you in your balls.

'I have confessed and am prepared for whatever God demands,' the Don muttered, and let his arms go, falling flat on his chin. He was upset enough to cry but the tears would not come so, bearing in mind that he was still within earshot of Lucille, he started to sob loudly and manfully and continued like this for some minutes.

'Pepe, I'm sorry. You know I didn't mean to do that.'

Saved from having to stretch his ham performance any farther, the Don got back on to his knees and wrapped himself in Lucille's bathrobe.

'Is it all right if I sit on your bed?'

'Yes, of course.'

For a minute the Don sat in limbo, angry that he had been reduced to acting in front of his daughter and unsure of which string to pull next.

It was up to Lucille to break the silence.

'Pepe, what *did* you dream about last night?'

The Don had no honest answer to this question. What's more he felt his daughter's tactic of steering the conversation on to a topic guaranteed to arouse his interest to be mendacious, smacking, as it did, of inherited insincerity.

'Have you forgotten?'

'What?'

'Forgotten the dream.'

He had not forgotten, or, at least, he knew but could not remember. The impressions were still strong but the chronology, plot, detail and meaning were all absent. He cursed himself silently for not airing his dreams over the dinner table while they were still fresh in his mind. It would have been better for them to have been dissolved in talk rather than to have disappeared into the unconscious processes they had arisen from.

'Are you all right?' whispered Lucille. She had stopped crying and now seemed aware that there was more than one casualty in the room.

'No, I'm not sure that I am,' replied the Don. 'My dreams, the dreams I had last night, they were . . . terrible, really terrible.'

'What happened in them?'

The Don sighed. 'It's very difficult to know how to start. I don't want to mislead you by saying the wrong things.' The room fell silent again. 'They're not difficult to explain, but they happened in pictures, not in words, and I don't know how to match the pictures with words . . . or to tell you what they meant to me.'

Lucille eyed her father cautiously. 'Try to, that's what you always used to say to me, try to.'

The Don hesitated, unsure of which strand to pick from the general picture of confusion he had helped create. 'I dreamt about the week in which I first met your mother,' he began tentatively.

'You mean the diving-suit story?'

'The week after the diving-suit story. I dreamt that I

entered your mother's house while she and her family were asleep. I watched her sleep, but I lacked the courage to wake her and, on leaving her house, a man approached me . . .'

'Did you know him?'

'In a way. When you were small, he was our cobbler for a while. But that happened in life. In my dream he walked up to me and said, "You know, there's a poem with the moon in the middle of it," and for some reason, in the dream, I was struck by the mystical significance of his remark.'

'Then what happened?'

'Well, then everything changed and I found myself in your mother's diving-suit, going down rapids in a kayak.'

'And then what?'

'Then nothing.'

'Nothing?' Lucille paused. Her father's dreams were full of too many feelings tied to too few events. 'I don't mean to be ignorant or disrespectful, but I don't see how this dream could have affected you in the way you claim it has.'

'That's because it has in a way that's not altogether obvious,' replied the Don quickly, angry that his attempt to take his daughter into his confidence had been thrown back in his face, 'in a way that involves déjà vus more complicated . . . more complicated than anything even I could grasp.'

Lucille nodded hesitantly. Her father looked like a man who had been tested and failed.

'And what about the other dreams, Pepe? I thought you said there was more than one,' she said for want of anything else to say; it already seemed amazing that earlier in the evening this question had interested her.

The Don looked at her blankly. His mind had started to work again and was displaying excerpts of the dreams he claimed he could not remember. Once again he seemed to be the victim of bad timing.

Lucille, sensing this distance, clasped his shoulder, but the Don was insensible, transfixed by the powers of recollection which were allowing him to re-enter his dream. The three great loves of his life had come to him: Lucille as a little girl, then a more mature version of what she would be like in a few years' time, another woman he did not recognise, and finally his wife. It was his wife as she was at the time of their first meeting, and his response to her arrival was electric. They sat on a gate together and talked. Everything he said to her was perfect, and he wished his words, and the seconds they were spoken in, could be preserved so he could share them with her when he woke up.

'Pepe, can you hear me?'

The Don faced his daughter but remained locked in his train of thought, for it was already upon him; the reason why his last dream had caused him such disquiet. The woman he could not recognise, who from time to time became either Lucille or his wife, had taken him to the edge of a beautiful canyon and, taking off her clothes, led him into a waist-deep pool, whispering to him gently all the while. But in the middle of this whispering there was something awful. Gradually the Don began to realise that the woman was telling him a story. A story about her friend introducing her to another man, a man who she was at pains to say she had no real feelings for but who, after a boring chat, had kissed her unlovingly. And once this happened nothing, not all the will in the world, could make things between her and the Don right again.

'Pepe, please talk to me.'

He had fallen into a terrible rage, and in the midst of it he had asked the woman awkward and painful questions that had made her cry. It was at this point that she had started to resemble his wife more and more as he repeated the same questions again and again. This scene continued as the couple moved through large libraries, summerhouses, allotments and department stores. But the argument in each place was identical, as was the rage that followed each question she could not answer. This continued until they arrived at the place where they had started; the beginning of the problem.

He did not know the woman in the dream. He did not know her because something in the dream had replaced a unique intimacy that had once allowed him real knowledge of his wife.

'The dreams were about your mother and me. I don't want to say anything else about them,' the Don stuttered.

The woman in the pool had wanted to make love to the man who kissed her unlovingly.

'Pepe, whatever it is, let it go.'

'Yes, you're right, I think I'll have to.'

The Don stood up and stretched his arms. The clock said half past three. It was time to let go.

'Yes, it's far too late for this kind of talk anyway,' yawned the Don, his tone affected but assured. 'It feels like we've had one of those conversations where we'll have forgotten everything we said in the morning. Goodnight, Lulu.'

'Goodnight,' said Lucille, tired and used to her father's way of coining nicknames on the spot.

The Don waved his arm good-naturedly, as if to hint to Lucille that she could discuss her problems with him any time she liked, and left the room.

As the Don walked back into his bedroom and got into bed he remembered that Lucille had been upset about something too.

'God, Rojo, you're a selfish bastard,' he mumbled to himself as he settled his head against his wife's arse-crack and closed his eyes.

Chapter Ten

2.55 a.m. – the Lower Tibidabo crossroads

Neither of the assassins knew the other and neither felt comfortable in the company of the other. Since both of them considered speech a sign of weakness, both had hoped the other would be the first to speak. Unfortunately, nothing during the evening had merited commentary and the silence, bar a few functional grunts, had held for over two hours.

This sort of thing was not normally a problem for the older of the two men. Once, when he was still a coach-driver, a friend of his wife had talked to him non-stop from Ronda to Vigo. She may have been trying to stop him from falling asleep at the wheel, but he calculated the problem to be simpler than that. She liked talking and he did not. The silence tonight had therefore come as a blessing, at least to start with, especially since the kid he was working with looked like a creep. But in the last ten minutes it had become a little too much and, he felt, had lasted a little too long. This put him in an awkward and unfamiliar position; one in which *he* was the one having to think of something to say. The younger of the two assassins, for his part, had felt like this all night.

It was the older of the two who spoke first, his question being, unsurprisingly, a practical one. 'Have I worked with you before?' He was glad he had got the words out, even though what he actually wanted to ask was whether the boy had ever killed anyone before. He would have had his reasons for asking this. His partner had thus far avoided playing a pivotal role in the evening's executions. This, in itself, had not been a problem for the first two executions. If anything, the boy would probably have got in the way. But in the third his help had been needed. Perhaps this was what had made the silence feel like it had gone on for so long.

'Why do you ask?' the younger assassin replied, sounding more insolent than he meant to.

'Because I like to know who I'm working with,' the older man said, surprised by the boy's confidence.

The boy smiled, raised an eyebrow and said nothing. In truth he was scared to say anything else; the older man seemed more like a policeman than anyone he could feel comfortable talking to. Maybe the old wart needed to intimidate people because he wasn't getting it from his wife at home, the younger man reasoned, pleased that at least, if nothing else, he was more perceptive than the older man.

The older assassin snorted knowingly and eyeballed the younger man, who now appeared to be ignoring him. It would have felt great to have fucked the flippancy out of the boy, but realising that he might be a little too old for that now, the old convict settled for spitting over the youth's legs.

'Two single-shot killings in that last job and you didn't so much as raise a fucking finger to help me,' he roared indignantly. 'You just sat here in the sidecar with both thumbs up your ass.'

The younger man smiled shyly. He was finding the older assassin's voice rather funny, now that he could hear it.

'You didn't even help lay their bodies out!' the older man continued.

Coming to the belated realisation that his partner needed humouring, the younger assassin put his hand on his knee and said, 'I was waiting for you to tell me what to do.'

The older man growled instinctively but, thought the young man, was noticeably softening.

'Well, we'll have to mind how we go once we're in the Rojos' house,' the older assassin muttered, losing some of his enthusiasm for his new-found capacity to make conversation.

'You're the man.' His partner smiled disingenuously.

The older man growled again, this time a little more affectionately. The boy was getting better but his instincts still told him that it would be stupid to rely on his partner too heavily. Ideally he would have liked to have taken a tumble with the boy to see what he was really made of, but he knew the timing to be wrong. Stopping the motorbike, he turned to his companion and said, 'Do you know how to drive one of these things?'

'I do.'

'Good. We'll swap places. You riding the bike, me in the sidecar.'

As they traded places, the older assassin felt himself give way to a thought he had been evading all night. His partner was trembling not with fear, but with excitement. In his lap lay a long sheath knife.

'I guess you're pretty handy with that.'

'Yes,' the boy answered, 'I am.'

The car stopped under the two fir trees.

'We're about two minutes' walk away from the Rojo hacienda now,' the Captain whispered dramatically.

Largo did not hear him. He was admiring his reflection closely, his expressions subtler than they had been earlier in the evening, his whole face beginning to emanate a rugged depth. This was certainly an improvement. The rear-view mirror on the general's car seemed to reflect a more flattering self-image than the one on the wreck they had abandoned earlier. It bolstered Largo's suspicion that high-class mirrors improved the looks of those who could afford to gaze into them.

'Largo, are you listening to me?'

'Uh . . . what?'

'Right, I'm going to go through this one more time. Largo, you and Josip are going to cut across those fields and come in around the left-hand side of the house. Josip will cut the telephone wires, but I want *you* to stop as soon as you get to the back door. That's where you'll stay until you hear me calling you. Fire into the air if anyone tries to get past you. Ali, you'll come with me to the front door. We're there to search the house if any one of the family answers it. If it's Rojo, we grab him and immediately double back to the car. Is everyone clear about that?'

All three men nodded. The Captain cleared his throat earnestly.

'Right. Once he's in the car, we'll take him as far as the *caballero* crossroads. When you swing left, Largo, Josip will crack off two shots as fast as he can, and I'll tumble the body out of the car. And that will be that.'

The others nodded again.

The Captain rubbed his eyes. 'I know we're all tired but if we follow this to the letter . . .'

'Where do we meet if anything goes wrong?'

'It's a set-piece act of two parts, nothing *can* go wrong. So long as everyone avoids improvisation nothing can go wrong.'

The Captain paused, but felt too tired to repeat such a simple plan. 'Okay, let's go.'

Ali blinked disappointedly. He had expected a bigger send-off.

'Wait a minute!'

'What is it, Largo?' There was concern in the Captain's voice.

'Um, no, nothing.'

'Well, come on, then.'

But it was not as easy as that. Largo could feel half

his body stopping to go back and the other half starting to go forward. He was not aware of having willed this, just aware of it happening. This was exactly what had happened at the barber's earlier that day. His whole being stalled and no one was taking the slightest notice of the change in him.

The other three men were already walking towards the Rojo house and, if he were to stay where he was, it would only be a matter of time before one of them would stop and ask him what the matter was. Automatically, incited by the preposterousness of this thought, Largo felt his legs advance at double time, as if through movement they could forget the worries that were beginning in his head.

Ahead of him the Rojo hacienda spread across his field of vision like a landscape he had grown indifferent to. Unlike the great sights of his childhood, which still seemed as large to him as they had on first entering his life, the Rojo hacienda meant less to him with each passing visit. He found his own attitude puzzling when taken in the light of his long history with the house and its surrounding grounds. The very field he was walking over was the one where he had first learnt to drive, his father, the Rojos' cobbler, balancing his tiny feet over the pedals of the Rojos' limousine. Largo stopped and looked around the field. If the experience in the car had contained a magic quality it had been lost somewhere; the field looked like nothing more than just a field.

Silently the other three men began to scale the shoulder-high wall that separated the Rojos' garden from the nearby paddocks. Largo, lacking the strength and height to do likewise, waited for Josip to pick him up and lower him over on to the other side. Although the wall had been built by Ali and Josip the summer before the war had started, Largo had helped them mix the cement and had engraved his initials into a brick. They were still there now. On the day of their engraving Lucille had offered the men orange juice which they had gratefully accepted, Josip more openly than the other two, Ali more sullenly and Largo with unrestrained, but clumsy, enthusiasm. Lucille's beauty, which often intimidated the three men, had on this day projected such sweet ease that all of them could have fallen asleep across the width of her smile. Later Largo had watched her sunbathe on what he had taken to be a large white handkerchief; he had stared at her until all he could see were the large sunspots that hung over her head like a protective cloud. Slowly a movement had begun in him, a movement which had yet to be stilled and whose primary consequence was a feeling of incompletion. This feeling had turned most of his world, especially that part of it that included the Rojos' property, into the lacklustre backdrop that had entered his field of vision moments earlier.

What frustrated him the most about this was the patent absurdity of the desire that lay behind his feelings. A desire that, if fulfilled, would grant him ownership of the Rojo hacienda, thus transforming it into a place that he could look at in *his* way and through *his* associations. This meant that the wall he had just been lifted over would cease to be a pile of bricks and would become instead a wonderful collection of stones, each one a magic component of a beautiful wall. If this thought was not embarrassing enough in itself, the one that followed it certainly was. This next thought mocked his pathetic ambition, mocked it for daring to be the same as everyone else's and, at the same time, for believing that the problem with the house and grounds was part of a larger problem that Lucille, or someone just like her, could provide the answer to.

His thought stopped talking to him. Hearing it in words for the first time was making him lose his balance. Its weight, heavier than the brain that formulated it, was starting to drive down into his guts, past the anxiety in his stomach, right through to the ground that held him up. Largo knew his only hope was to ignore its force, accept its tense sickness, and carry on walking. To listen to such a thought would render him as immobile as he had been in the barber's when Lucille had cut his life short with a few arbitrarily chosen words.

Blinking nervously, as if he were still facing her, Largo attempted, for the second time that night, to derive a lesson from what Lucille had said earlier that day. His effort was sincere, but partly wasted, as her closing words had made him forget a great deal of what preceded them, leaving him with no clear picture to mull over or understand. His habit of understanding meaning through pictures, and not through the language used to carry them, left him stranded when faced with a meaning that did not lend itself to visualisation. Usually this did not bother him, quite the reverse, it provided him with less to care about whilst offering the opportunity to laugh at those who *did care* about what they could not understand. That *he* could ever one day be in *their* situation had been too ridiculous a scenario to contemplate.

But now it was his turn.

The light in the barber's had extended as far as the window would allow it, which was as far as the counter but not as far as the back room. Lucille had come into the shop to settle her father's monthly account and had not noticed Largo, hidden under the till. Still half asleep, on account of the bender that was still continuing in the back room, Largo had huddled up in a protective ball and listened as the barber apologised for the noise coming from his son's enlistment party. Lucille had looked at her watch in mock outrage and the barber had laughed. It had, he'd agreed, been going on for a long time and would soon be winding up. Just so long as it wasn't on her account, Lucille had sighed gaily, before adding that there were things about men that only women could understand but that there were also things about men that only other men could understand, and drinking at eleven in the morning was one of these. The barber laughed again, this time a little sycophantically, and complimented Lucille on inheriting her father's wisdom as well as his good looks. Using this as his cue, Largo had got up and walked around the counter, coughing loudly and feigning a bruised hangover. Lucille's greeting was at once amused and cordial. Largo, confronted with something as simple as a greeting, had no idea how to respond. Her voice had affected him too much to reply with a greeting of his own, but beginning his day by telling a girl how lovely her voice was struck him as awful. It was far easier to ignore her altogether. His surliness had amused her even more, causing her to ask why, since they both knew each other, he found this simple fact so difficult to acknowledge in a greeting. Thrown, and suddenly aware of how difficult it was for anyone to say anything to anybody, Largo had grunted and, with calculated lack of interest, muttered something about not getting on with women.

'Well, you're stupid, then,' Lucille had said. 'You're stupid, Largo, and you're a coward.'

At first all he could hear were these words but then, at the pace of a funeral procession, the world had stopped happening for him. Minutes passed before the world had started again, by which time Lucille had gone and the Captain and Josip had emerged from the back room. It was already too late to say anything or to wonder whether there was anything that should have been said. He had just stood there before quietly joining the others, who were drinking at the counter in silence.

A silence not dissimilar to the one he was following them in now.

Lucille gazed at her handwriting. It was not like that

of the other girls. Its style was more like a boy's, with each letter at odds with the shape of its neighbour. As no letter ever resembled itself, a reader could be forgiven for thinking that Lucille had never learned to write properly, each of her inscriptions resembling her first efforts at putting pen to paper.

The fact that Lucille was incapable of joined-up handwriting had been much to the Captain's taste, this supposed flaw making her other perfections more human and grounded. The two had engaged in a lively written correspondence, which Lucille now found herself trawling through. Amongst the postcards and letters were much shorter notes dating back ten or more years. These had been dropped on her desk during bright spring mornings to a backdrop of Latin and science. The notes themselves were surprisingly surreal and almost wholly uninformative, allowing Lucille to be as interpretive as she wished on returning to them through the years: 'Lulu, the draught looks like it's frozen your fingers, you ought to be in gloves anyway. It's getting colder and Tonio's head keeps getting in the way . . .' It made her wonder who she was, what sort of person it was that the Captain had been writing to . . . 'I'm bored. Wink twice, you irresistible sauce.' And she had. The girl the Captain had fallen in love with had worn long grey socks, buckled sandals and hair held up by a wooden pin. Her head would bend over her desk, a closed smile would spread across her face. A reply would be composed.

The all-pervading sound of her father's snoring

moved through the otherwise silent house. Whenever this had occurred in the past it had been accompanied by a feeling of tender sympathy. But now it seemed strangely distasteful, unwholesome even. Attempting to ignore it, she turned the old note over in her hand. The Captain's old address was scrawled on the other side in imitation of her own writing. Nothing will look so sad as that name written in my address book and me remembering the euphoria I felt as I first wrote it down, she had thought at the time, and she had been right.

Her father's snoring was growing even louder, forcing her mind back to more immediate concerns – feeling sorry for her father being less indulgent than her own melancholy. The evening's activity aside, the Don had, for some time now, become a figure of steadily diminishing proportions. 'Steadily' was the correct word, as Lucille was never consciously aware that she had started to think less of her father. Scratching her nose, she tried to locate the source of the rot. Had the Don begun to repeat himself too often, snore too loudly or bore her? Was it because Rosa had walked into the observatory and witnessed the foulness of the Don acting on his own lust unaccompanied and promptly told everyone she knew? He was certainly guilty of all these things, but the slow change in Lucille's feelings had a much simpler source.

Lucille was old enough now to see her father as others saw him, and try as she might she could not unlearn this knowledge. Not only did this mean that his unique place in her life was lost for ever – he was now one father among millions and not the only father in the world – but her truth grounding had disappeared too. His wisdom, and all wisdom, now seemed open to question. Since none of this meant she loved her father any less, her former respect for him had been converted into a strange but intense sympathy. As he seemed unaware of any change in the relationship, Lucille felt that telling him would be unnecessarily egotistical (her feelings for her father had changed, so what? People are dying every day, she could almost hear him say). If he was in a more reflective mood he would probably put his interrogation hat on, try to reduce her to tears and demand to know the cause of the change. And this was a potentially embarrassing subject. It concerned advice she had not asked for, but nonetheless had acted upon: boyfriend advice as supplied by the Don.

The Don's attitude towards her boyfriends had always been ambivalent. Under the familiar maxim of only wanting the best for her, careful holes had been torn in her judgment, the Don only just stopping short of destroying her confidence completely. By the time the Captain arrived on the scene, the Don was ready for a challenge, the competition accelerating in proportion to his daughter's love for the boy. Despite making little headway, the Don watched vigilantly for any rift or lovers' tiff he could exploit, and it was during one of these that he had offered his daughter the following advice: 'Love for a particular type of woman is over once she is able to recognise a man other than the one she loves as beautiful.'

The circumstances that impelled him to offer this advice were, needless to say, tenuous. He had overheard Lucille agreeing with her sister about the good looks of one of the newer boys in her class. This remark had occurred during a period of considerable turbulence in her relationship with the Captain, and the Don had seized upon it as only an embittered old man could. Incredibly, and to his own surprise, he was successful. It was the last time the Don would ever be able to convince his daughter of something so completely. She had agreed with his insight: it was *true*, she could have eyes for other men. Why, she asked, should she suffer at the hands of someone she only *thought* she loved, and the Don had nodded approvingly at the use of this careful psychological distinction.

But the advice, of course, had failed to hold up, and the Don's reputation for wisdom had suffered a similar fate. Sensitive to this, as he was to all things, the Don had gone on the attack and attempted to consolidate his advice with less specific philosophical musings: 'I know that breaking up is about as close as one can come to death without actually being killed but believe me, you've done the right thing, and would you like to know why? Because you've been brave enough to learn a valuable lesson. You now know that people who love one thing too much don't understand the valuelessness of everything, something you *must* understand if you are ever going to love *one* thing well.' Slowly, however, it occurred to him that he may have overplayed his hand and that, although nothing had been said, Lucille was not listening to him any more. So without wasting too much time doing penance, the Don had picked up from where he had left off and carried on as if nothing had happened, if just because he did not know what else to do.

When, some months later, Lucille had heard her father concluding an exchange with his brother with: 'There are some people who admire the glass, and then there are others who are able to see through it to the other side', she had not known whether to laugh or cry. This was the third time she had heard him use that aphorism in a month. It was as if she had been living under the warmth of an artificial light. Her father was full of shit and she was over him now.

The Don had stopped snoring and the first birds had begun to sing. Lucille eased her shoes off and fell asleep fully clothed.

Chapter Eleven

3.30 a.m. – a paddock behind the Rojos' house

Whistling quietly over the early morning wind, the younger assassin allowed his partner to carry on with his painfully delivered speech. The older man had spent the last five minutes whispering colourful gibberish in an attempt to impart some semblance of a plan. The younger assassin had not listened to a word of this but had been careful to provide the appearance of having done so. It was not that he was scared of alienating his partner; far from it, he felt perfectly qualified to see the job through alone if he had to. Rather it was the pleasure he derived in leading people to believe he respected them, and could learn from their knowledge, that let him humour the old man without interrupting. Other people's delusions fascinated and comforted him, both for their sake and his own, and the excitement he derived in encouraging others to be pompous, and the pleasure he took in debasing himself in front of their 'superior wisdom', bordered on the ecstatic. He had never questioned why this was so, and would probably have found himself answerless if he had, but there was no questioning the number of opportunities other people gave him to practise this bizarre vice. Smiling patiently, he let the older assassin finish whatever it was he was saying, shook the man's hand firmly, and darted out of the undergrowth into the open field.

Approaching the Rojo house, by the side entrance, and not through the back door as the older assassin had just instructed him to, the young assassin started to assess what was in the evening's work for him. He had got as far as the two Rojo daughters before he realised any further deliberation was unnecessary. They would be enough in themselves. The rest, their mother or whoever else there could be, was a bonus. There was no point in being too greedy, there would be plenty of time for that when he got older.

Trying the handle of the side door, and finding it unlocked, the assassin let himself into the kitchen and helped himself to a glass of water.

Ernesto and Alcazar went on alone. The half-tracks were to follow them if they had not returned in an hour.

'We'll give it an hour, then once we've woken him up we can enjoy a chat with the bastard,' said Alcazar, and laughed slightly unconvincingly. His manner seemed to have lost some of its naturalness and his attempt to compensate for this was making it even more strained.

'Do you think that . . .'

'No, I don't. I don't think he's in any danger at all tonight, just that he might be if he goes on the way he is – which is why we all need to chat.'

'I admire your confidence but I'm afraid I don't share it, I've a feeling that everything's wrong . . .'

'If there's any trouble I'm sure we'll be able to handle it.' Alcazar grinned. 'And besides, I live for trouble,' he said jokingly, pulling a face which made Ernesto laugh, not least because it looked like the face of an occupational troublemaker.

Alcazar shook his head and tutted familiarly; he was feeling a little better.

The stretch of road they were walking along was one the two men knew well. As children they had organised themselves into gangs and held huge fist fights which had lasted whole summers along its banks. Alcazar had led the gang from the outskirts of the city and the Don had been the head of the one from the surrounding countryside; in the end numbers made the difference and Alcazar's pack nearly always won. This had, in Ernesto's opinion, given Alcazar his taste for deeds over abstraction, and taught the Don he was a better thinker than fighter. As such, Alcazar now tended towards mental sloth, denigrating most things that were not of immediate use, while the Don had become unhealthily self-absorbed. Ernesto, who had never tended towards extremes, had continued to mediate between their two egos in the role of second fiddle ever since. For the first few years this had meant being the middle man in their conflicts and constant flare-ups but, since they had turned fifty, it had involved growing accustomed to the hurt pride and wounded egotism that had silenced their friendship. He believed that, for once, the blame for this lay more with Alcazar than his brother. The Don at least acknowledged there was something wrong – Alcazar did not. For him, the fact that he had not talked to the Don for a long time seemed a good enough reason to continue to not talk to him. There was also a matter of having to identify what the problem was; and this hurt Alcazar more than the Don since he was loath to take pathetic things seriously and all his arguments with the Don *had* been pathetic.

Ernesto sensed that his companion was about to say something. Picking up a stick and swinging it playfully, Alcazar announced, as if to himself, 'At what stage *exactly* do you think the Don became such a windbag?'

'What do you mean?' asked Ernesto unnecessarily, aware that he was being put in a position in which he could only sound conciliatory and, to Alcazar, foolish.

'What I mean is that, for someone who had so many premonitions of how to avoid becoming a gasser, that is before he became one . . .'

'You mean that Braulio always said he'd do everything he could to avoid being swallowed into the system and its procedures?'

Alcazar looked as though he were about to burst out laughing. 'Yes, that's the sort of thing I mean. Supposing he was serious then, given that, it seems strange to me that these premonitions came to nothing.'

Ernesto replied as though he were thinking aloud: 'I think the premonitions, on their arrival, terrified him.

But by the time they came true he was so used to them that he didn't care.'

'So you wouldn't contest the fact that politics broke him – making him even fuller of shit than he was in the first place?'

Ernesto winced. He disliked Alcazar's way of describing anyone moderately intelligent as full of shit.

'You won't get me to badmouth my brother, Raul,' said Ernesto defensively, before adding quickly, 'You were the only one to realise your childhood dream. By the time the rest of us grew up our dreams had changed. You were lucky, yours stayed the same.'

Alcazar tutted facetiously. 'I was only asking if you thought he had become a bit of a donkey.'

Ernesto blushed, ashamed that his much-remarked-upon fault of wishing to 'intellectualise' things had once again been brought to the fore.

'The way I see it,' Alcazar continued, revelling in his own directness, 'is that you've got to have a lot going for you to be such a pompous ass and the Don hasn't got enough, and, if you ask me, he never has had enough to walk the line he does.'

Ernesto offered nothing in the way of a reply. He had heard it all before. For someone who claimed to despise rhetoric Alcazar was nothing if not repetitious, and the decline of the Don was one of his favourite, and most thoroughly rehearsed, subjects. Ironically it was because of this that Ernesto had turned to Alcazar for help, calculating that Alcazar's bluster was born out of admiration for the object of his attacks.

The two men walked on in silence until they reached the entrance of the Rojo hacienda. The ground was uneven and potted with rainwater in every hole. Alcazar eyed Ernesto carefully, aware that it was his job to say something next. For a moment he hesitated, mindful that he had harmed too many friendships by trying to break up awkward silences created by his deliberate facetiousness.

'So here we are again,' Alcazar exclaimed with a smile. 'Let's see what you've got left in the tank. I'll race you to the back door!' And they began to sprint down the drive.

Josip enjoyed the climb up the telegraph pole, happy that he could still treat life like such an adventure. It made him proud that he could still experience things like an eleven-year-old but understand them like a twenty-four-year-old man. The dullards were the ones who understood life like children but experienced it like adults. He was relieved to be just as he was but frightened as well, frightened that things would change and force him to be different.

Josip took off his cap and stuffed it into his belt. The cold morning air hung gently over his head, calming him and allowing him to notice more of the surrounding country than he otherwise would. He liked the vantage point provided by the height and the way the moon illuminated his view of the Rojos' house. It gave the air a strange quality that reminded him of chalk and staying up late when he was small. Quickly he thought of his own three children and wife but killed the thought before it could go anywhere; they, and the thought that carried them, belonged to a different part of his life, and it would not do to bring them into this one. It made him uncomfortable to think about how deeply he loved them and, because of this, he took care to not mention them in front of the others or even think about them too much when in their company. His reasoning was that if they were not talked about no one else would have an opinion on them and, more pertinently, no one else would have the right to judge them. Besides, he always felt guilty bringing them up, as if he were trying to prove something that should, on account of its truth, be passed over in silence. In any case he was no saint, his lingering affair with Muerta was evidence of that, and he did not want to sound like any more of a sanctimonious hypocrite than he already felt he was.

Josip wriggled his way up so that he was just below the top of the pole. He was roughly level with the top floor of the Rojo house, four storeys in all, he estimated. Gently, he eased himself farther up the pole.

Without meaning to, his thoughts had returned to what the Captain had said about murdering Rojo. He was angry with the Captain for reminding him, or for perhaps making him realise, that he was here primarily for the money. Money was not his principal motive in life but the cash he would receive for killing the Don would help his family in ways he hadn't even had time to think about yet. Whatever else the money would do, it could act as a much-needed short cut to the kind of security he would never get from a thousand years of serving in the army.

Resting both elbows on the top of the pole, Josip hauled the rest of his body up so that he was sitting astride its summit.

It was a shame that they were going to kill the Don, it really was, but it was one of those things that just had to be done. He had never had much to do with the Don but what he did know of him was mostly bad, and besides, he didn't like the sight of him strutting around and generally acting like one of those bastards who went around believing everyone respected them all the time.

Strangely enough most people seemed to, but Josip, described by the Don as a natural anarchist on account of his dress trousers being too short for his legs, knew better than that. The remark had come at a government function where Josip was acting as a waiter, and had provoked great hilarity amongst the Don's audience. The Don had even taken a mock bow and invited his listeners to applaud Josip, who stood fastened to his post, balancing a tray of champagne in each hand. The incident told Josip nothing that he didn't already know but unfortunately still fell short of providing a personal motive strong enough for him to want the Don dead. Even the things that had happened in the last year had failed to convince Josip that life was cheap, and unlike many of his friends, he had been unable to accept the casual and cavalier attitude towards killing that was current practice. His objections, though from the heart, were probably not as deeply held as those of the Captain, who thought that something must be learned from every death. Certainly he could learn from the death of his mother, but it seemed too much to expect him to infer anything from the countless battlefield corpses he had encountered. He could leave that to the Captain . . .

Josip took his wire-cutters from the satchel.

Ali had shot Salazar, and that hadn't been a bad move. But Don Rojo was different. To start with he, as he had already established, lacked sufficient motivation for this killing. Money was not enough. Without it, he would be killing on behalf of someone else's motivation, which struck him as dishonest. If pushed he could think of reasons for killing the Don, but the point was these were not *his* reasons, or, to his mind, *good* reasons. They were ultimately shallow and not as deep as death, things about the Don he had come to accept from the outside, from watching what a silly cunt the man could be. Whether the Don exploited farmers, scored points off waiters, accepted bribes and had threatened to defect did not, when all was said and done, really concern him. It was not his call. This was not his war. And yet, perversely, it was Josip's cheerful temper and sense of ease that allowed him to move so freely with the flow. That and his friendship with the Captain – a vain fool but his oldest and dearest friend.

Josip cut all four wires and took one last look at

the tops of the trees. It would be forty years before he would see them again, forty long years in exile, at the end of which he would return to this spot and attempt, in front of a camera crew, to recreate what he now saw. And silently he would ask himself, *Why can't I talk to any of you tonight*, and answer, *Because none of you are here.*

Getting off the post, far faster than he had climbed up it, Josip positioned himself next to a bush and signalled to Largo at the back door.

Largo waved back and held his nose. What provoked him to do this was a mystery, as the Rojos' garden was as fine a place as any he had smelt. Perhaps the misguided desire to impress and amuse was at work again. In order to mitigate or justify it, Largo yelled in what he thought was a hoarse whisper, 'The dustbins out here stink of shit!'

Josip flared up as if he were about to charge him and ran his hand across his throat to signify silence. Largo, trying not to laugh, hopped back and fell straight into the back door, bouncing off the woodwork and nearly knocking himself out in the process.

A light came on upstairs and both men fell flat on their fronts. There was a smash of glass from the other side of the house and another light came on, followed by a woman's screams.

Ali and the Captain did not hear this or, if they did, did not react to it. In Ali's case this was almost forgivable and, if the Captain had been more alert, the signs would have been obvious on Ali's face. This was only the fourth time Ali had stayed up all night and he was exhausted. Adrenaline had kept him going as far as it could, and shooting Salazar had probably given him an extra hour, but the relative warmth of the car had been too much, and now he was beat. It had taken him a while to realise that he was so tired that he was not even scared; his eyes were dry and sore but his nerves were perfectly calm. This, at least, was a gentle consolation of sorts.

His walk up the drive had been as straight as that of a sleepwalker, his face unblinking and expressionless, able to look but not see. The rest of his body was relaxed to the point of uselessness. Stumbling clumsily, he felt his ankle twist. The pain was sharp enough to wake him and restore an overall sense of awareness. He could feel his feet now and they were wet, whether through rainwater or sweat he could not tell. Nor could he understand exactly where he was, his body having woken from its deep numbness, and thus robbing him of all illusionary orientation. Panicking, he thrust his head up and sprang on to his feet like an athlete at the start of a race. He must not lose sight of the Captain. Holding both arms out in front of him, like a mummy, Ali quickened his pace and tumbled straight into the Captain, who had paused a few inches away from the Rojos' front porch. Noiselessly the Captain grabbed Ali, drawing his head up to his face. 'What the hell's the matter with you?' he whispered hoarsely.

'I . . . I fell asleep, I think,' Ali stuttered.

In the dark Ali could just make out the outline of the Captain's face; he seemed to be staring at him in horror.

'Please,' the Captain implored, his voice heavy with worry, 'please don't do that again tonight.'

Ali nodded obediently, his face flushed with embarrassment.

The two men resumed their journey to the front door. Ali could feel his ankle reverberate with pain but it was his head that was worst affected of all. His mind had as little in common with what his body was actually doing as his fantasies had when masturbating. Both seemed focused on different activities. His body on making the Captain think it could keep its balance and his mind on Lucille Rojo. There was nothing strange in the choice of the subject matter, but the direction his thoughts were going in, to say nothing of their unprecedented speed, was quite new.

He had written a letter to her that he was now carrying in his breast pocket; its content was an eclectic mix of adolescent effluvia, part love letter and part self-justification for the projected murder of her father, the Don. His intention was to leave it somewhere in the house where she could find it. Then he could return to the house in a few days, once everything had blown over, to see what sort of effect his words had had on her. But the letter, written boldly and simply, he believed, already seemed strangely unrepresentative of his feelings.

Rather than a vehicle through which love expressed

itself, Ali now wanted the letter to be more questioning, or, he hoped, able to answer a question that had just occurred to him. Why did he want Lucille for ever, and why had he always assumed that the answer to that question was self-evident? After all, he had never shared any kind of life with her, or even spoken to her for more than a few minutes. Instead he had comforted himself with the thought that the Captain and Antonio were his curators – looking after her until it was his turn – and it was this 'comforting' assumption that now seemed so questionable. Everything may come to he who waits, but once it had, would he still want her, a girl he hardly knew? It now struck him that he had fallen, and remained, in love with a single moment in time, and that the essence of that moment, Lucille's soul, had stayed still whilst he had moved on. And as he moved, he had faithfully carried and created this moment in memory, all the while distancing himself even farther from its actuality. So when he now looked for it, there was nothing there. He no longer loved Lucille Rojo, and he did not know what was going to happen next.

Ali brought his hand to his face and stifled the urge to be sick. The truth was that he did not know what he thought. So much time had been wasted ... He loosened the hold of his gun-belt across his stomach, the bent holster slipped to one side and his revolver fell to the floor. In a few minutes this would cost him his life.

Speaking through his teeth, so as to avoid hearing himself cry, Ali whispered up to the Captain,

'Francisco, if love isn't active any more, but there's still plenty of love there, then what is it?'

'Are you having a laugh?' hissed the Captain mechanically. 'There is a time and there is a place!' He was tired of these sorts of questions. Ali was always asking them and no sort of answer ever seemed to stem the tide. Intensely fond of him as he was, the Captain did not have enough respect for Ali to make an effort at a moment like this.

Holding back his tears, Ali whispered an apology and let the matter drop, sure nonetheless that if it had been the other way around he would have answered the Captain's question.

Unlike Ali, the Captain was very much awake. His blood was up and his heart felt like it was falling down a spiral staircase. What was he doing here? The question was as belated as it was foolish. This was what came of answering questions before they had even been posed properly; of thinking things would be easier to do when put on the spot. Volunteering to kill the Don had been the most impulsive thing he had ever agreed to do in his life, but, unfortunately for him, the moment of the impulse had already passed. The Captain glanced over at Ali, who seemed to be drifting between a coma and a trance. The situation was becoming unnerving; what if the same thing was going through his friend's mind? But so what if it was? It was not the situation itself that was working away at them like a wound; it was what had brought them there.

The Captain was not as scared of killing the Don as

he was of meeting Lucille again. He had slept heavily in the afternoon and the past few hours had been spent dwelling in the ache his dreams had left in him. This was the source of some anger, as he disliked dreams and had often denigrated Lucille for the amount of emphasis she placed on them. As with everything he had been wrong about, things had come full circle, and now it was his turn to mull in infinite, painful and unproductive self-analysis. Fortunately, as he was close to becoming sick with himself, there was not much of his dream to remember and therefore little to recount.

It could not have lasted for more than sixty seconds and involved only two emotions, indignation and love. The indignation, at least, was relatively simple to understand. The Captain had dreamt that he had caught Largo impersonating him in the middle of a monologue that was embarrassing enough to have come from his own mouth: 'The first and only time I have ever experienced love has been in its unrequited form. This pattern has continued to the present day, with each successive love being more half-arsed than the one that preceded it.' Recognising that it was his pain that was being ridiculed, the Captain had moved to strike Largo across the face. But Largo, with his finger over his lips, had pointed to a cot in a corner of the room. In it Lucille lay asleep with her legs dangling from its sides. The Captain did not want to wake her too quickly – he wanted the moment, a moment which he felt as if he had spent years waiting for, to be a *memorable* one. *He could still feel her eyes opening when he woke up.*

The Captain shook his head, embarrassed at the force of his feelings. Seeing her face again would not solve any of his problems. Nor would trying to remember what it was like to sleep in the same bed as her. He would run up against the same limits that he had run up against when he was with her. The only way he was going to change her life, and his own, was by killing her father. And that was what he was here to do.

It was from the other side of this thought that the Captain heard the breaking glass and the woman's scream and, for a fatal moment, he, like Ali, failed to react.

Antonio came to with a shake; he could hear tapping on the window. His first instinct was to get up, put his clothes on and leave. The instinct was strong, but he did not obey it. He was comfortable as he was, lying in Rosa's warmth, experiencing something new and nearly perfect. All this ought not to be given up for instinct alone. But the rapping or, to be more precise, grappling on the window ledge was getting louder. Quickly untangling himself from Rosa's sleeping embrace, Antonio drew the curtain far enough to see a set of long white fingers pressing gently against the glass. Before realising it, he was once again in the grip of instinct. In seconds those fingers would be part of a larger body moving through a broken window.

Without pausing to wake Rosa, Antonio slipped out

of bed, wrapped a towel around his waist and was soon in the hall tiptoeing down the steps. Only when he had reached the bottom of them did he question why he was in such a rush to get away. Again, his brain worked quickly and automatically, so geared was it to the business of self-preservation.

The facts were simple, even if they were still unclear: someone was attempting to break into the house – at best to burgle it, at worst to kill its occupants. The only thing that mattered was to get out, to put distance between this place and himself. And yet he hesitated. Somewhere in the recesses of Antonio's being, the small voice of conscience was competing, with other louder voices, to be heard. He could not leave Rosa like this.

Antonio glanced up at the staircase. There were a lot of steps on it. He *could* leave Rosa like this. For some people, it is not difficult to be true to themselves. For Antonio it was especially easy.

Leaving through the door was too risky. It was almost certain to be watched. Far better to crawl through the bathroom window. Silently, Antonio crept up to the bathroom door. Beside it was a row of hooks, but none of them held the coat he was looking for. It was, he decided quickly, better to be killed in a towel he was already wearing than to be found dead in the morning wearing a shopping shawl. Beneath the hooks was a mounted photograph of Rosa on a horse. For a second, Antonio thought of helping himself to it. After all, if the household was to be slaughtered, who would notice a missing photograph? On a second's further reflection he decided to leave it where it was. It was better to take nothing that would connect him with the house. Besides, the photo gave him an uncomfortable *presentiment* of the future. He could just see Rosa in a few years, surrounded by friends, running him down for his cowardice, and all those slags nodding sympathetically and saying, *Yes, we could have told you. He was always like that.*

'Trollops,' he muttered under his breath, and tucked the photo and frame into his towel. Prising open the bathroom door, he fumbled around for the sidelight switch.

He had made a mistake. This was not the bathroom. It was the kitchen, and he was not the only person in it.

Antonio paused and then doubled back through the hall into the downstairs bathroom. Arriving where he had intended to, but by mistake, forced him to catch up with a situation he was fast losing sight of. There was definitely something wrong, of that there could be no doubt, but whatever was wrong was not happening as quickly as he expected it to. In other words there was still time for him to work this situation to his advantage. Moving impulsively, and knocking over the tortoise that Rosa kept in a bucket of water beside the toilet in the process, Antonio found himself charging up the steps, this time not making any effort to be quiet. Before he knew it, he was standing outside Lucille's room, pushing her door open. She was lying with most of her clothes on, fast asleep and oblivious to his presence. On the floor, next to her bed, was an old cigar box and, surrounding it, thousands of tatty old letters. Antonio had never sent anyone a letter in his life so he knew they could not be from him. Picking up a pile hungrily, he began looking for his name. But it was not to be found. Instead what was common to all the letters was the signature at the foot of the page, Francisco Sabate Liopart, the precious twat otherwise known as the Captain. Antonio felt his blood drop and rise at the same time. If there was one guy in all the world he hated it was the Captain. An evil, egotistical bastard he would happily kill if only he thought he could get away with it.

Antonio quickly checked the date on the letter he was holding; it was written within a week of the Captain and Lucille breaking up.

'. . . I can't ever feel secure about it because of times like this. This thing means that it can never be taken for granted. No matter how good it ever becomes again . . .'

What the hell was the Captain referring to? Antonio licked his lips and glanced up and down the page. The answer was disappointingly mundane.

'. . . your temper terrifies me. It lets you down and stops you from being yourself. I want to give ground to you but I know I can't because you'll piss all over me . . .'

Antonio raised an eyebrow and nodded. He was not above feeling a strange kinship with the Captain. The guy obviously knew what he was talking about.

Without knowing why, Antonio took the letter and laid it out on the bed beside Lucille's sleeping body. Then, having put the rest of the letters back in the cigar box, he made his way back down the steps and crept into the kitchen.

He smiled automatically at his bad luck.

There were now two people in the kitchen. And one of them was carrying a large knife.

Once in the kitchen, Helena Rojo realised that the voices she could hear were coming from outside the house. Trying to see through her sleep, she peered into the garden. Slowly, she made out the shape of a man's head and shoulders and those of another man, much smaller than the first, crouching only a foot away from the back door. The two seemed to be communicating in some kind of sign language, and, judging by what she could see of their faltering movement, were probably drunk. What they were doing there she did not know or even care to know. Probably soldiers lost on a manoeuvre, or local boys hoping to spy on her sleeping daughters. In truth, Helena Rojo did not have many thoughts that were not connected to her husband or daughters, and those that she did have did not occur to her at five in the morning. Finishing her glass of water, she turned to leave the kitchen, still half asleep and dead to the world.

Inches away from her face, the younger of the two assassins fingered his knife nervously. His stomach was burning with excitement. It felt like he was about to steal something and get away with it. Grabbing Helena Rojo firmly by the hair, he pulled her down on to the floor and jammed his knife through her neck. To his surprise, this occurred soundlessly. He repeated the movement, first once, then twice, then once again because he liked the way it felt.

Just a foot away, Antonio Mayle stood motionless, certain that he was about to die next. Holding his breath, he shut his eyes and waited to be killed. But it didn't happen. The assassin did not seem to notice him, so involved was he in his immediate task. Moving as though he were avoiding a fall, Antonio turned the latch on the back door and crept into the garden. Directly in front of him, facing the other way, was a dwarf he immediately recognised as Largo and, for the second time in as many minutes, Antonio found himself rooted to the spot. The situation was saved for him by the sound of breaking glass.

After much ado the first assassin had finally eased his way through Rosa Rojo's window. This exercise had taken twice as long as he had intended it to, partly because he was out of shape but also because of fear. Not fear for himself, but for his partner; the idea of setting him loose in a house full of women was not one he was comfortable with. Still, he had no choice now. Lowering himself off the ledge, the assassin felt his foot sink into a mattress. He froze. Just his luck to land in the imperial bedroom.

'Antonio, hmmm,' muttered a voice.

Without willing it the assassin found himself moving the wrong way, as he hitched himself back on to the ledge and attempted to survey the scene dispassionately. The fact was that without his reading glasses he was practically blind in this light.

'Mmmm, Antonio, let's do it all over again . . .'

The assassin toyed briefly with the idea of breaking her neck, but dismissed it at once. Was it because he didn't have it in him or because he had forgotten how to? His silencer was in the sidecar and, as a rule, he did not like to kill women with his hands. This was not the fault of morality; if anything was to blame it was his time with the Legion in Morocco. There, he had found that killing women close up had brought out a side in him he did not like.

'Mmm, yes.'

But here she was, waking up right in front of him. He would have to do something; it was what he was here for, after all.

Reaching around for Antonio and not finding him, Rosa got up in such a way as to be facing the assassin head-on.

'Antonio, is that you . . . what are you doing up there?'

Instinctively, the assassin recoiled so that the weight of his body shifted from the ledge to the half-open window. Not only had he lost his ability to act decisively, it also looked like he had picked the wrong room; this was a girl, too young to be Rojo's wife.

'What are you doing up there, Antonio?' asked Rosa, and reached up to touch the man who was blocking the moonlight out of her room.

Instead of grabbing her wrist as he had intended to, the assassin flinched even farther, losing his balance completely. With an almighty crash he fell backwards, diverting his fall so that he tumbled sideways, shattering the jarred window into tiny fragments. Rosa screamed and turned the light on.

The scream was loud enough to wake the Don, who was left in no doubt as to what it meant.

'So, they have finally come to kill me,' he announced to the place where his sleeping wife should have been. 'The important thing now is to avoid any unnecessary bloodshed,' he continued as he got out of bed and put on his robe. 'Life just is, then a moment later it isn't,' he mused aloud as he crossed the hall to Rosa's room. Both his mind and body were tense with excitement; it had been worth waiting for. It would be decided tonight, he would either live or die. If they failed tonight they would not try again. He had spent a long time preparing for this moment, or at least, if not preparing for it, then certainly thinking about it. In the past his chosen means of dying had always involved leading a doomed but glorious cavalry charge, but, in recent years, he had come round to the more realistic prospect of being murdered for his politics. This meant an execution, preferably in public, where his last words would be recorded for posterity and crowds would stand in awe of his courage before the scaffold.

He paused.

Perhaps he was ignoring the obvious. That the reason he had always fantasised about scenarios leading up to his own death was because, in the last instance, he knew he would fuck up the real thing.

The length of hall connecting his bedroom to Rosa's was pitch black, and the Don thrust both of his arms out in front of him like a blind man. This made him doubly unsure, both of himself and of his self-image in the face of death. If anyone could see him through the dark, he realised, what they would see was not a charging dragoon, but an injured footballer committed to a half-hearted tackle.

With a thump he felt his leg swing into something crawling around his feet.

'How long have you been down there, Rosa?' stuttered the Don as he helped his daughter off the floor.

'Just these few seconds,' his daughter stuttered back.

Chronologically, this made sense, but it would not have surprised the Don if she had been there longer. It had always been in her nature to watch others from dark places. The creepy indignity of waking up to find her standing over his bed had led the Don, earlier in the summer, to adopt her trick and spy on her. Concealing himself in her cupboard, he had, somewhat absurdly, waited for her to come back from school. She had duly arrived with a friend in tow and launched into a bitter diatribe aimed at the Don, culminating in the description of him as the father of all wankers. The Don had waited to feel the heat of his wrath swell up, but nothing had come. Instead, he made himself even smaller, waiting a full hour before tiptoeing out of his hiding place. He had thought he had known his daughter, but her words had revealed the existence of a parallel life; a life in which she was capable of uttering such words, a life completely at odds with anything he had thought or felt about her. His favourite maxim had proved to be a sham: 'If I can't say I know that girl then I can't claim to know anything'. Since that day Lucille had re-established her position as his favourite, and Rosa had been relegated to a puzzle that kept him up at night.

The Don felt his reminiscence stop itself and throw up a new thought that ought to have occurred to him earlier, much earlier. How far had things come if he was reduced to hiding in his daughter's cupboard to access information? He shuddered. If this was the man Rosa had come to know, it was no wonder that she considered him little better than a common masturbator. The Don wanted to tell her about everything he *had* done, and *had* been, so that she would know what he was really like, but the conclusion was already stronger than the solution; perhaps he had been a wanker then too, or, worse still, a tosser.

Behind him he could hear the sound of feet rushing down the steps. It was Lucille. The Don smiled happily, pleased with haphazard chaos unfolding around him. Nights, for him, tended to be a series of ups and downs, but this one was turning out to be a bizarre sideways movement. His smile broke into a grin. He could hear men yelling at each other downstairs. His belief that everything was unbelievable until it actually happened seemed, once again, to be receiving its ultimate vindication in life.

Turning to his two daughters, the Don whispered authoritatively, 'Both of you wait here and don't move from the top of the steps. If anything happens wake your mother up, tell her that I love her, and then hide. I'm going downstairs now.'

'Did you hear that?'

'I'm not sure. Did you?'

'Listen . . .'

'I heard *that*.' From the far side of the house, the sound of a man in terrible pain could be discerned.

'Shall we go and look . . . ?' Ali could feel his shoulder blades clatter together like cymbals. Just to his right was a large window flanking the front door. If he had known what to look for he would have seen movement on the other side of it, but instead he chose to stare at the dark bulk of his own reflection. Staring as hard as he could, he tried to make out the reflected image of his own eyes, calculating that if he could see them, all would go well tonight.

'Ali, just get inside,' whispered the Captain violently.

Panicking, Ali redoubled his efforts to catch sight of the centre of his eyes, terrified now of the stakes he had attached to the success of this task.

'*Ali* . . .' The Captain was pushing his back.

It was no good, his pupils were elusive. 'It's just fuckin' superstition anyway,' Ali uttered like an embittered drunk. Throwing the Captain's hand off his back, he reached up to the doorbell.

'What are you fucking doing?' the Captain cried in exasperation. 'Just force the fucking door open, quickly.'

Ali pushed the door open and stumbled into the Rojos' hall. Right ahead of him was a man he half recognised as the Don walking down the main steps. Ali felt as though he should say something, but his feelings, if functioning at all, were not working in language. Reaching for his gun, he found his holster upside down and empty. 'Shit,' he thought. 'SHIT!' he heard someone else roar.

'AAARGHH!'

Rolled on to the floor, Ali felt like he had been caught up in a great blast of wind. One that was heavy enough to carry another man with it. His legs felt like they had been sliced off at the ankles. Blood was gushing in spurts from his chest, forming rhizomatic tributaries either side of his insensible body. *What the fuck*, he thought, *has just happened to me* . . .

Ali came to with a sigh. He was still bleeding and still on the floor. Strangely the thought that he might not be, that he might be safely tucked up at home in bed, a natural enough thing for a man in his position to think, did not occur to him. Instead he found himself worrying over whether Lucille would be able to read the letter he had prepared for her. That he would be alive to give it to her, of that he had no doubt. The trouble was the state the letter would be in by the time she received it. It was not the sort of letter he wanted to write out twice but he was well aware that he might have to. Blood was moving through his vest into his inner tunic pocket and, from there, into the top left pocket of his new flak jacket. He groaned. That was where the letter was. Neither jacket nor letter would come good for him now.

Just ahead of his eyes he could perceive an animated line of energy hurtling one way and then the other. It was, in actual fact, the Captain attempting to wrestle a large carving knife out of the hands of a boy in a blood-soaked tunic. Pinning, with a mixture of rage and deliberation, the boy to the bottom of the banisters, the Captain began to shout at Ali. Ali smiled. The Captain wanted to know whether he was okay.

Rosa watched the two sets of three things happen at once. First her father froze, as two men fell through the front door and another stumbled in from the kitchen. Then all three men were on top of each other, there was some shooting from outside and her father was, before she knew it, walking back up the steps again. It was, she felt, turning out to be a very exciting night. Grabbing Lucille in a sisterly embrace, she squeaked, in a pitch higher than anything she had ever heard from herself before, 'It's fucking madness, isn't it!' Lucille blushed and returned her hug with a reproving, but in the circumstances utterly absurd, truism: 'Don't squawk so loudly, they might hear you.' Looking up the stairs, the Don shrugged his shoulders and smiled nonchalantly. His daughters smiled back.

The man on the steps had changed direction and behind him Ali could hear the sound of raised female voices. Whether the man was or was not the Don did not matter now. Instead Ali concentrated on the girls' voices. They felt reassuring, like the sound of passing traffic during an afternoon nap.

Having straddled the assassin, and knocked the knife out of his hand, the Captain had begun to beat the boy's brains out over the foot of the first step. Ali watched him approvingly until it was too difficult to keep his eyes open. He didn't see the Captain stopped, before he could finish his task, by the sharp muzzle of a gun pressed against the back of his neck.

The first assassin had always enjoyed boasting about his high pain threshold. The boast was based on coping with hangovers, the number of press-ups he could do when drunk, even arm wrestling and the occasional fist fight. None of these, however, had prepared him for the fall from Rosa Rojo's window and the attendant pain that now spread through his body with the force of a claw hammer. He was, high pain threshold or not, bearing up to it very badly. At least no one could see him, he thought, by way of consolation, but this thought brought with it a more worrying one, which was that he had not fallen silently. Buttoning his lips with some effort, he struggled to get back on to his feet and limp his way free of the shattered debris in which he was covered. His pain was quickly turning into anger, the kind born from repeated, and humiliating, frustration. The job would still have to be completed; they had wasted a lot of time and lost the element of surprise, but that was all. The whole house would know he was coming now so it was important for him to get to them before they came looking for him.

Stumbling around to the front of the house, as fast as he was able to, the assassin pulled out his pistol, resolving to use it as soon as he could. He would not get caught being 'kind' again. Finding the front door open, he hobbled in incautiously. For a second his attention was distracted by the sound of gunfire coming from the other side of the house, but the sight before him demanded more immediate attention. By his feet lay a dead soldier covered in stab wounds. Stepping over the body, the assassin drew level with the head of a second soldier, who appeared to be attempting to kill his partner.

'Stop what you're doing and freeze like you're having your picture taken.' Pressing the muzzle of his revolver into the back of the Captain's head, the assassin glanced up and saw a figure moving slowly up the steps.

Hazarding a guess, as neither the dead man nor the one he was pointing the gun at seemed to fit the description, he shouted, 'On the stairs, if that's you, Rojo, you can come back down here.' The figure on the stairs stopped, turned around slowly, and began its regal descent.

Switching his attention back to the Captain, the assassin hissed quickly, 'Now get out to your left, soldier, and stand absolutely still. I want to forget about you for a while.' Pausing, to release his breath, the assassin briefly examined the state of his partner on the floor, before asking, 'Are you alive?'

'In theory I am,' the bleeding boy cried back.

'I asked whether you were alive,' the first assassin repeated, completely deadpan. His confidence was returning and the pain from the fall had now progressed from anger to jubilation. It was just as well since, as usual, it looked as if he was going to have to do everything himself. He felt his balls tingle with excitement. This was just as it should be.

The boy got up holding his head in both hands and rocked it up and down to answer in the affirmative. His previous swagger was now entirely absent.

'Good. You're not as hurt as you think you are, though God knows you deserve to be. Pick your gun up and search the rest of the house. I want to get this over with quickly.' The assassin glanced up and down the hall furtively. What were these soldiers doing here and where was the rest of Rojo's family?

'Where do you want me to go?' the boy muttered pathetically through his hands.

'Upstairs. I'll deal with things down here. And hurry,' the first assassin said, and added, 'I think I can hear shooting outside.'

Chapter Twelve

From the moment Antonio had seen Largo, any thoughts of this being 'his night' had been dispelled. The two recognised each other immediately.

'It's you,' Largo yelled disbelievingly. '*What the hell are you doing out here?*'

'What the hell are *you* doing out here?' Antonio fired back, not so much interested as amazed at such improbable bad luck.

Before he had time to hear an answer, he was back on the floor again, the full weight of Josip bearing down on his body.

'What the hell are you doing out here?' Josip breathed down his neck.

'Get off me, you fucking fool,' Antonio snapped. The impact of the fall had knocked his towel off and, unsurprisingly, he felt vulnerable in his nudity.

'Tell me what you're doing out here and I will,' growled Josip, seemingly oblivious to both the erotic and comic implications of lying on top of a naked man.

'Isn't it obvious?' intervened Largo, grinning apishly, instinctively at home in another man's misfortune and

217

yet keen to help if he could. 'It looks as though he's out for a spot of skinny-dipping.' He laughed, kicking a clod of earth into Antonio's pained face.

'If you let go of me I might be able to tell you something that could help you,' Antonio groaned from under Josip.

'If that's true then why don't you tell us what it is now?' said Josip.

'Shhhh, what was that?' wheezed Antonio as loudly as he could. 'Didn't you hear it?'

Leaning to one side, Josip temporarily lifted the weight of his body off Antonio's back. Seizing his chance, Antonio sprang up and darted forward, losing both his photo of Rosa and Josip in the process.

'Jesus Christ, there's nothing covering his buns,' gasped Largo, waving Antonio's towel in the air. 'He's galloping away in his birthday suit!'

Josip turned to register the fact, but instead saw two clothed figures running as fast as they could towards the front door. Antonio, only too aware that he was as naked as the day he was born, now found himself trapped between more hostile parties than he cared to count.

'Who the fuck are they?' shouted Largo and, remembering something the Captain had said in their 'briefing', pulled out his revolver and fired two shots over the heads of the running men, who seemed to be in the process of racing each other.

Aborting their race, Alcazar and Ernesto threw themselves to the ground in a synthesised movement heavy with conviction. Lying flat on his back, with his face to the stars, Ernesto tried to catch his breath. Next to him Alcazar, wheezing noisily and splattered in mud, unfastened his pistol and returned fire in the general direction of the house. The oncoming fire did nothing to prevent the panic, which was serving as Antonio's guide as he launched himself through the alternating trajectories of bullets, hopping wildly like an animal trapped in a fairground target range. Without his realising it, the direction he had chosen was leading him straight into the laps of Alcazar and Ernesto.

Diving from the slight indentation of gravel that was acting as cover, Alcazar pulled Antonio down by the legs and pinned him flat on his face in a puddle.

'What's happened to all his clothes?' asked Ernesto, more shocked by Antonio's nudity than by the two men firing at them.

Wrinkling his forehead, Alcazar struggled to suppress a smirk. 'I don't know what kind of house your brother's running these days but this is real prize-winning stuff! Look at the boy's feet – they're fucked!' Alcazar laughed, pointing at Antonio's bleeding toes. 'Maybe this runaway is who you should be addressing your questions to. Perhaps he knows who's firing at us and what's going on in the house, eh, Romeo?' Alcazar nudged Antonio playfully in a way that he hoped would encourage a rapport.

Unable or unwilling to answer, Antonio ignored the overture, struggled back to his feet, and carried on running. Shaking his head with a mixture of mirth and curiosity, Alcazar let him go.

It felt as if he were in flight, that he would stop running when it was time for him to land and not when he was too tired to go farther, for Antonio was already very tired. Nothing he was running from meant anything to him; all things existing as little more than colours and shapes he had to get past and escape. Of his feet he felt only a thick pain; like his heart and lungs, they seemed to be serving no purpose other than to impair the speed of his flight which, after five minutes of running, had covered an impressive distance, if at a high physical cost. For a young man who could usually be relied on to flinch if a single hair was out of place, Antonio had truly entered a new mode of being.

It was this inattention to anything other than his rapid escape that allowed Antonio to ignore the troop of soldiers who were slowly advancing up the road. To ignore their amused but utterly pitiless faces, as the corporal leading the troop yelled to the others, 'You're not going to believe what's coming bare-arsed and straight at us . . .'

For if he had not ignored these things, he would have thought better of his line of flight and turned back, at the same speed, towards the relative safety of the Rojo hacienda.

This thought would, in hindsight, occur to him more than once.

*   *   *

Grabbing Largo by the collar, Josip hurled him through the kitchen door and into the house. It was imperative to link up with the Captain and Ali immediately now. Behind them a well-aimed bullet ricocheted off the woodwork of the swinging kitchen door. The first thing either of them noticed, once inside, was the freshly mutilated body of a woman. The second was the gun levelled at them by the first assassin, who, by now, was wishing he had arrived with more men.

'Drop your guns and come into the light slowly.'

'What's that doing there?' Largo asked, pointing at the dead body with a foolish enthusiasm.

The assassin brought his gun hand down on to the side of Largo's head with considerable force, his eyes still firmly trained on Josip.

'Now drag him into the hall, slowly or I'll shoot you both.'

Josip obeyed the command. The assassin, despite his advanced age, was now emanating a practised ruthlessness that left both Josip and the battered Largo feeling out of their depth.

'I said slowly, but not that fucking slowly. Hurry up with him, take him up by his collar.' With his head bent down, Josip tugged Largo behind him, their inability to exploit a numerical advantage transparently obvious in his burning red cheeks.

Moving as slowly as he could, Josip shuffled Largo into the hall and took his place next to the Captain and the Don. They were backed up beside the second assassin, who was watching them from the stairs. At a nod from the older man, the second assassin departed from his charges and, with some of his old hunger, cantered up the steps towards Rosa's bedroom.

The Captain watched him go with increasing disbelief. If Don Rojo was on the eve of defecting to the fascists then what were two of them doing in his house pointing a gun at the old man? Was it possible that they were here to protect him, or perhaps this was some kind of show being enacted out to make the defection look more convincing? The Captain could feel his own reasons for being in the house shrink under the shadow of a larger story which, though as yet uncomprehended, was competing for validity with his own. To his left Ali lay perfectly still, his body a static rock in a river of moving blood. This was, the Captain knew, his fault. If he was too shocked to grasp this fact now, the emotional content of the event would be sure to hit him later on. If he was still alive.

The assassin glanced at all four men nervously. It had just occurred to him that he did not know what to do next. The situation had seemed controllable when he had first walked through the front door, but now there were men appearing from everywhere. His strength lay in the fact that none of them could know who he would shoot first if they tried to rush him. This, however, was only a temporary advantage. Cursing himself, the assassin realised that he had left it too late, he could not shoot them all at once, but (and this was the real problem) with them all bunched together it was impossible to pick them off one by one. If he realised this they would too. Reality was unfolding faster than his mind was able to, thus transforming what was happening around him into an unrealistic situation – one that he could soon lose all sight of. In the hope of buying precious seconds in which to decide what to do next, he said, addressing Largo, 'You, half-pint, what are you doing here?'

'We're Don Rojo's bodyguards,' Largo fired back, hoping to buy precious seconds of his own in which Josip and the Captain could work out what to do next.

'How many of you are there altogether?' asked the assassin, already calculating that if he shot the Don, and somehow was able to make it obvious that it was only the Don he wanted to shoot, then, luck willing, the other three might not rush him at all.

'Just us here,' the Captain said, staring the assassin straight in the face so as not to have to look, or think any more, about Ali's dead body.

'You speak when I tell you to,' spat the assassin, horribly conscious now of where the first signs of trouble were likely to come from. The emerging danger was that if he tried to buy time, in which his partner could come down and help him kill these fools, he was also wasting the time he needed to make a clean getaway. He had broken, and was in the middle of breaking, every rule of an execution. But once the first rule was transgressed, that is, to kill everyone as you find them, a situation like the one he was now in was unavoidable. The assassin turned to the Don who had, since reaching the bottom of the stairs, stood in impassive silence like a statue. Through some deep intuition, the assassin could perceive the Don as emerging as some sort of saviour of the situation but . . . He stopped himself. What the hell did he think he was trying to do by making things so complicated? He was wasting precious seconds. Glancing quickly at his watch, the assassin saw his fear confirmed. It had been twenty-five minutes since they had parked the bike and sidecar on the edge of the Tibidabo road, leaving plenty of time for it to have been discovered and dismantled.

Returning to Largo, the assassin said, 'Don't come the old soldier with me. I know that where there's some soldiers there're always others.' He was thinking of the half-track he had had to circumnavigate to get to the house. 'I want to know how you got here.'

'On four wheels.'

'Well then, that's the way I want to leave,' the assassin announced impulsively. His partner, who obviously preferred to try his hand with the ladies rather than help him down here, would have to take his own chances. It was every man for himself now.

'To get out of here you'll need to get through at least three, maybe four roadblocks,' interrupted the Captain, guessing the line the assassin's mind was working along. 'To do that you'll need us alive. Not just a driver but all of us, they'll expect all of us to be in the car. If we're not they'll hold you until they find us . . .'

'Why would I need him?' protested the assassin, who

was starting to feel that by not shooting the Captain he had already agreed to too much.

'Which of us do you mean?' asked Largo helpfully.

'Him, of course,' the assassin said, pointing at the Don.

All four men looked at the Don, who seemed to have been forgotten in the excitement of their collective arrival. Staring at him made the Captain think of Lucille. In his daydreams he had always hoped to perform some great feat of bravery in front of her, preferably to save her life from a masked gunman. Now that destiny had handed him his chance the Captain could see that any heroics would not occur within Lucille's field of vision. The first thing that had to be done was to lead the gun-wielding maniac out of the house. For that to happen it was in all their best interests for the Don to stay alive, for the moment, since it was now perfectly clear that if the Don was defecting no one had told the fascists. As for the other assassin upstairs, the Captain felt sick with shame and helplessness. Lucille and Rosa would have to, for the moment, look after themselves.

'You haven't answered my question. What's to stop me from killing this one now?' shouted the assassin, waving his gun at the Don. The Don, for his part, looked neither scared nor brave; nor even interested. Close examination of his lips, however, revealed a man who was praying silently. The assassin brought his gun up under the Don's chin and cocked the trigger.

Josip clicked his tongue; the assassin's game was

obvious enough, and simple to see through. First he shoots the Don, then he kills the officer, then he asks Josip what's to stop him from killing the dwarf, then he gets me to lead him to the car and then that's that, Josip thought, game over. He stared down at Ali's dead body. In the minute since he had first walked in he had not even noticed it, he had not even wondered *where Ali was*. But he could not afford to grieve now or give in to the fatalism that usually overcame him in times of danger. It was wake-up time or die. 'Wait!' he and the Captain cried at the same time. The assassin stared at both men and both men stared at each other. Josip nodded at the Captain and said, 'People are already on their way round now to see if he's all right. We were first in a group of twelve. Take him *with us* and then you've got cover.' The assassin withdrew his gun from the Don's chin. There was still no sign of his partner, and he was now sure that if he shot the Don, with one man down, the other two would charge him down on instinct, if nothing else.

Pursuing the thread of his story, and deciding against telling the assassin that the Don was, in any case, meant to be defecting, on the grounds of how implausible it would sound, Josip continued with increased confidence, 'We can say, when we're stopped by the others, that we've been following orders and taking the Don to Nou Camp for his own protection. They'll buy it if we play it like that but we need the Don with us for it to work.' Josip stopped himself, unsure whether he could follow his logic to its conclusion. He had come here to *kill* the Don, and now he was trying to save his life, even if it was for his own ultimate gain. Maybe I'm not a bad guy after all, he thought quickly, before continuing, 'Once we're out of here you can do whatever you like to him.' He gestured at the Don. 'All we want to do is to leave here with our lives.'

'Why should I believe you're telling the truth?' asked the assassin, aware that the initiative was already being transferred across the room. 'You're his fucking body-guard, for Christ's sake, his trusted men,' he sneered.

'Do you think any of us want to be sent to the front to be killed?' yelled Josip, certain now that whoever had been firing at them outside had nothing to do with the man currently pointing a gun at them inside, which, in the short term, gave them a distinct advantage. 'Do we look like we haven't had enough?' he added with a ghastly expression that bordered on a parody of fear.

The assassin edged backwards. The only thing he was now sure of was that he wanted out too. 'Hey, upstairs,' he called out to the second assassin. 'Upstairs, can you hear me?' he called out again, wishing to God he knew the man's Christian name. There was no reply. He knew his voice would have carried throughout the whole house. He was on his own. The two and only important things were that there should be no witnesses and that he should live to see daylight. The psychopath upstairs would kill anything in his path; that was unfortunate but also useful. And when they caught him, as they undoubtedly would do, they would kill him well before they got round to questioning him.

There would be no witnesses. All he had to worry about was what he saw in front of him. A collection of desperate cowards and a mad old man.

'Okay, you, half-pint, open the front door and the rest of you get ready to follow him out.'

Suddenly it occurred to the assassin that he had forgotten something. 'Wait, stay where you are. There was shooting outside earlier. What did it have to do with you?'

'That was us just letting off a few rounds to scare you,' answered Largo, edging open the door and wondering from which direction he would be shot at first.

'How many of them are there?'

'I can't see properly. Only one, I think.' Alcazar was agitated, torn between his instinct to charge into the house outnumbered against a prepared enemy, or to do what he had actually done, which was to sit tight and wait.

'Should we fire?'

'No, not yet. It's impossible to get a clear shot in, with a pistol anyway.'

The two men had sought cover behind a large pine tree overlooking the Rojos' front door.

'Here we are, they're all coming out now. Two, three, four . . . four . . . no, five, five of them.'

'Can you recognise . . .'

'Your brother's with them. They're holding a gun on him . . . If we fire they'll kill him outright, and it looks as though they outnumber us two to one.'

'I'd rather do the wrong thing than nothing,' said Ernesto, who had become increasingly martial over the evening.

'No, no, that wouldn't do any good. Far better if I track this lot and, if I need to, try and lead them towards our men. But I don't want you coming with me.'

'Why not?' Ernesto protested, affronted at the challenge to his new status as front-line soldier.

'Because there's a family still in the house and someone needs to check on them. Besides, there might be even more men in the house.'

'Which way should I go in?'

'Try a side door. They may still have someone watching the front entrance.'

Ernesto nodded obediently and scuttled along the same path Josip and Largo had used twenty minutes earlier. Alcazar raised his eyebrows silently. Ernesto's white panama jacket and riding breeches were, even in the bad light, a dark shit brown. He had never seen his friend so filthy or, for that matter, so undetached. It would be nice to think that later, once they were in the warmth, Ernesto would thank him for the experience.

The structure of the house shook with the force of the closing door. Now the only sound the two girls could hear was the second assassin's breath rising and mingling with their own. He was very close. Under her bed, Rosa curled herself into a small ball. She could sense his presence in the room now, and she knew he was likely to find her sister first. Lucille was hiding in the cupboard, an obvious place for her to hide and for him to look. The assassin clutched his face and emitted a loud groan which echoed through the house as loudly as the Don's snoring had an hour earlier. He knew they were in here. He had seen them at the top of the stairs being shooed away by the Don, and heard their protests as they were told it was for their own safety. There was not enough time for them to have hidden properly. They would be in the first room they had come to, which was this one. Lurching forward, the assassin threw off the duvet and thrust his knife into a pile of pillows. The angle of his movement, and the absence of the intended target, affected his balance and he tripped forward over the bed into the wall. His head felt the same way it had done when as a child his sisters had swung him around the garden. The room was rolling and pitching around as if he were on board a ship, and the open wound carved across his head was starting to bleed again. Gently, he ran his index finger along the indentation of the wound and held it up to his face. The finger, and his whole hand, was covered in what looked like red oil. If he did not find these girls quickly he would pass out. This knowledge restored his balance and in a second he was back on his feet. Biting into her arm, Rosa tried to make herself even smaller by shutting her eyes tightly. A tactic similar to hiding under her covers from witches and wizards. Unlike the latter, however, its efficiency was about to be tested.

Swinging around the room, the assassin let out

another groan, louder than the first, and sank to his knees.

'Just come out, and I'll let you go,' he lied. 'All I want to do is see if you're all right.'

Rosa knew that this was not all what he would want to do. She also knew that if she were to live then she would have to take matters into her own hands. Firmly placing the scissors she had grabbed off the worktop between her thumb and forefinger, she rolled silently on to her front. The assassin's ankles were only a few inches away from her face. At the count of two she would stab them. Two seconds passed and nothing happened. She willed her arm forward but it would not move. Her whole body tingled with ecstatic frustration. Again she counted to two and again nothing happened. Her volition, like mucus, slid down her throat and upset her gut. She was useless. Though no more useless than her sister, who, at that moment, was pressed up against the boiler, her knees level with her face. The crack in the cupboard door was wide enough for Lucille to see the assassin hovering between the bed and cupboard. In the half-light she could make out the features of his beady face, young, very thin, but haggard in a scarecrow-like way. It occurred to her that she had seen him before, perhaps at a school sports day or at work in one of her father's fields.

'I'm going to count to ten, and then if you don't come out, I'm coming to find you.'

Lucille felt as if she were ignoring a boy who was staring at her, or about to tell a man who would not leave her alone to go away. But these analogies presupposed a response, and this was a situation that would not allow for one. She would never see her father again, and he would not see her. She could still hear his desperately mumbled parting, delivered as he doubled back down the stairs: 'Go to the one you can tell everything to.' For her, this person was the Captain. She had realised this as she watched him struggle with the gunman at the bottom of the stairs and decided then that if life had a point, he was hers. But it was already too late to tell him. He was with her father now, and she was by herself.

'Ten!' barked the assassin.

'Two!' screamed Rosa, and swung the point of her scissors into the assassin's calf. His screaming was so awful that it sounded exaggerated as he tumbled over into the doll's house, breaking its roof into two. Flailing his arms and legs wildly, he lashed out against the anticipated second assault. Finding it not forthcoming, he attempted to use a nearby shelf to lever himself off the floor, but instead brought its full weight down on his head.

'Hold him where he is and I'll stab him again!' shrieked Rosa as she emerged from her hiding-place, a second wave of courage spreading through her as she nearly tripped over the assassin's tangled legs.

The assassin could feel her abrupt movement, and that of another body springing out from the cupboard. He laughed . . . Let them kill him, it might be even more fun this way around.

Grabbing his ears with one hand, and his hair with the other, Lucille wheeled him into the centre of the room, where Rosa waited with the large knife he had dropped. Tearing open his shirt like a surgeon performing an emergency operation, Rosa jammed the knife into the folds of his stomach and carved into his groin.

'I'm not sorry,' she whispered.

Lucille let go of his ears.

A moment or two passed and the two girls sat looking at each other.

'I don't know about you but I'm not going back to bed,' Lucille said at last, certain, before she had even finished speaking, that she meant something much more than this. Something had changed in her life and something else had finished. From now on she would no longer puzzle over colours, number games and other carnival distractions. Instead she would look to her heart and live.

Resting against Rosa's bed, she watched her sister get up and leave the room. Outside, the light was already turning from dark blue to white.

Chapter Thirteen

_____

4.40 a.m. – side entrance to the Rojo hacienda

Ernesto Rojo found the back door open. The air in the kitchen was musky and raw, identical to that of the sacked village he had entered earlier that morning. Making the right connection, he found himself scanning the room for signs of death. Helena Rojo's body was in the same state as the assassin had left it. Taking off his jacket, Ernesto knelt down beside it and draped the garment over her mutilated throat. Surprisingly, her face looked unaffected by her body's pain and she wore a maniacal frown, which seemed more comic than sincere. Despite this, though, this face's resemblance to his brother's wife was troublingly inexact. The face Helena Rojo had owned in life had been led by the most tremendous and unaffected smile Ernesto had ever seen. This smile was the device which allowed all men to love her at a distance, the one part of her that exceeded her restrictive and all-consuming love for the Don. But the expression she now wore reminded Ernesto of Helena's outward adherence to formality. It was a formality that strangers often found intimidating, but Ernesto saw it for the foil it was; the straight man for her far greater love of play.

And now there was only this face.

Ernesto kissed her forehead gently, feeling slightly ridiculous as he did so. It seemed too trite a gesture given the finality of the occasion, and its clumsy insignificance forced him to face down a cliché he had long thought he had got beyond: *What is the point of loving life for years and years if, on one night, everything can be undone like this; better never to have known joy or love at all than to continue in life without either.*

Coughing violently, Ernesto stumbled to his feet, uncomfortable that life was transforming the heart of this cliché into a viciously pure truth. Carefully, he closed the lids of Helena's eyes. At least, unlike earlier in the village with Alcazar, there was no one here for him to share his mute and life-denying shame with. At least he was not expected, as a man of *words*, to *say* anything.

'Uncle?'

'Rosa . . . ?'

Rosa peered down at the body and, as she had with the assassin, looked at its deadness for a moment. The past few hours had led her to believe that, awful as they were, they had at least rid her of her talent for tears. She had even gone so far as to wonder whether, as someone who was now completely incapable of crying, she would ever find an equivalent outlet to tears through which to release pain. She need not have worried. Within seconds she had lost all semblance of emotional control. It was true that she had been cured of tears: tears shed for herself, but not those shed for others, and especially not those shed for her mother.

Their noise, pure as it was, somehow missed the point, thought Ernesto as he continued to stare into the face of his dead sister-in-law. Her frown now seemed the prelude to a smile and, in a strange way, she seemed to be telling him that she was still the same. Very gently he ushered Rosa out of the kitchen and closed the door behind her. Picking up Helena's body, he carried it into the garden and laid it down in the morning dew. Somewhere in his mind was the resolve to bury it before sunrise.

An hour later, Lucille found him fast asleep by the freshly dug grave, her mother's body still wrapped in a coat beside him.

Alcazar saw the five men get into the car and pull out from under the fern trees. There was something disjointed about their overall appearance, and only one of them actually seemed to be holding a gun. Alcazar snorted, removed his pistol from his holster and tucked it into the back of his trousers. Then he released his gun belt and threw off his cap. The cool morning air was becoming heavier, the first forecast of a hot day. Without moving, Alcazar watched the car hit the track, gather speed and leave him behind. He snorted again, this time a little madly, and, with a cavalier smile pulled for no one other than himself, sprinted after them as fast as he could.

* * *

'Just keep driving straight and don't stop until I tell you to, roadblock or no roadblock.'

Or until you drown me, thought Largo. The assassin was sweating hard enough to suggest that he had just returned from a swim.

'Anything you say, sir,' said Largo, before adding, quite unnecessarily, 'You're the boss-man.'

The assassin started as if to say something, but remained mute, unsure of how to respond to what he had just heard. In normal circumstances he would just shoot the man, but the moment for that had already passed and, besides, the dwarf was driving the car.

Unable to believe the extent of his own sarcasm, Largo continued: 'Yes, these are the strange hours. Not night, but not exactly morning either . . .'

'Shut your mouth!' barked the assassin, once again in possession of speech.

Turning to Josip, Largo smirked. 'This guy's a real arse-haulier.' The two men burst out laughing like boys in detention, knowing that they would be told off, and that this made the situation even funnier.

'Are you both crazy? Do you think this is some fucking joke?' yelled the assassin, lifting his pistol away from the Don's side and waving it at the front two seats, where Largo and Josip were sitting, to make his point.

Josip stopped laughing and bent round. The assassin, who was in the process of unleashing a new wave of sweat, snarled, less convincingly than before, 'Don't you understand that I could kill you?'

Josip, who was really past caring now, nodded with shocked mockery. 'I'm sorry, I guess it's the fault of our nerves, we were up all night guarding that old bastard.' He pointed at the Don.

'The night's been very hard on all of us, Josip, this man doesn't need to hear all about our problems,' pitched in the Captain, not clear whether he was meaning to be funny or not.

'Do you mind if I put the radio on?' asked Largo. 'It might help us all to calm down a bit.'

'I will shoot the next person who says a word,' said the assassin with as much conviction as he could muster. He must have been crazy to get in a car with all *four* of them, he thought, as he glanced nervously at the Don, who was sitting to his right. They weren't cowards, *they were fucking mad.* Each one and without exception, *mad.* He should have at least killed *one* of them before they got into the car, preferably that lippy young officer. Instead he was now sitting squashed between two of them, with only a gun pressed into the Don's ribcage for comfort. This would be scant consolation if the other three now decided they were less interested in the Don's wellbeing and more concerned with the idea of avenging their dead friend. What was preventing *them* from killing *him*?

The assassin quickly surveyed their respective faces. It was difficult to tell who he hated most, let alone who he would have to kill first. The preening officer, who was even now checking his reflection in the rear-view mirror, was a younger version of the Don, that much was obvious. As such, he and the Don deserved to die at the same time. The assassin gently felt his inside pocket for the reassuring shape of his second revolver. That said, the tall cunt in the front was not much better, just better at containing his insolence, and that was all. As for the dwarf behind the wheel, *who was practically having to stand behind the wheel*, the assassin sighed in disgust. The dwarf was a sign of the times. All of these scum were.

Largo sat up with a start, met the Captain's eyes in the overhead mirror and winked. The Captain winked back. Largo sat at ease. They had won. This clown was exactly where they wanted him to be. It even looked as if he would kill the Don for them . . . that is, if they let him. Peering out of the corner of his eye, Largo caught Josip's smile. It made him feel strangely free and brave, brave enough to do anything he liked. If that sweaty cunt's pal could kill Ali then they could most certainly kill him, he thought, as he slowly began to speed up the car.

If Largo, the Captain and Josip were beginning to enjoy a more relaxed mood, the Don was suffering from just the opposite. He had not uttered a word since the assassin had first drawn his gun at him, and he knew this indicated to the others that he had given up, that the real Don Rojo was as powerless as he was weak when faced with the great leveller – the loaded gun that was now pointed at him. The only thing that could be said for this shame was that it was not as bad as the knowledge that lay beneath it – the knowledge that told him he would die this morning just as surely as it had once told him he would marry his wife and become the president of the Cortes. It was a knowledge imparted to him from his mother and given to her by God – a God he had scarcely given a thought to in years.

Thank you.

'What did you say?' asked the assassin.

He had always known he had taken greater pains in revealing himself to the Lord than the Lord had in revealing Himself to him, though never had the Don been more aware of it than now. Nor had he ever wished so hard for the Lord to give a little back and never, in the act of wishing, had he been so unsuccessful in concealing the anxiety that marked the space his wishes would arrive at.

Please . . . Please speak up . . . Please . . .

'What the hell are you talking about?' the assassin yelled weakly, now sure of his initial estimation that he was the only sane person in the car.

'What the hell is he talking about? If this is some kind of cock-eyed signal I'll shoot you first, you smartarse prick,' the assassin shouted at the Captain.

Leaning over the assassin, the Captain took the Don by the head and stared into his eyes with genuine curiosity. The Don's long face looked sick and overstretched, giving the impression of a man who had withdrawn a long way into himself. It seemed certain to the Captain that the Don was completely oblivious both to his situation and their presence.

'I don't know what he's talking about and that's the truth,' said the Captain with calm satisfaction.

'It's obvious, isn't it, he's lost his fucking mind.' Josip laughed, clearly enjoying this latest confusion.

The assassin lifted his gun over his lap so that it was now pointing at the Captain. His hands were so wet now that he was afraid the revolver might slip through his palms. If he were honest with himself, and there was no point in not being, he had lost any real conception, if he'd ever really had any, of what he wanted to do next or where he wanted to go. If they came to a checkpoint, all any of his passengers had to do was wink and that would be it. Why couldn't he have seen that in the first place? It seemed so obvious now. None of these soldiers could be trusted and they all seemed to be getting braver by the minute. Maybe his best chance was with the Don, maybe now was the time to explore his first strange intuition and turn to the Don as an ally.

'Listen, Rojo, there's still a way for us to get out of this alive . . .' the assassin screamed like a madman. 'Listen to me, damn you, I can save your life!'

But the Don heard nothing. Instead he felt a great calm come over him, reminiscent of the feelings he had experienced ever since childhood when he was late for school or for an important appointment. This calm was always greatest when haste was what was most required of him, and it would grow in proportion to this urgency.

'What are you going this way for, and why so fucking

quickly?' shouted the assassin, who had temporarily abandoned thoughts of pursuing a tactical alliance with the Don, once he'd realised that Largo had taken the car off the main road.

'Because of that,' Largo shouted back, pointing at the half-tracks that blocked the road ahead.

'Drive through them,' screamed the assassin.

Ignoring him, Largo hauled his tiny body up and dropped the full weight of his foot on to the accelerator pedal. The car broke forward like a racehorse and all five men were thrown back. Grinning manically, Largo, leaning on the wheel to stay upright, turned it at a right angle, sending the car on a new course down the bank that sloped to the side of the track.

Meanwhile, back on the road, the first rays of sunlight burnt through the clouds into the half-tracks that formed the roadblock, creating a wall of reflecting steel. The light was blinding.

Foaming at the mouth with aggressive confusion, the assassin threw his firing hand up and stuck his pistol against Largo's head. It was time, oh yes, it was at last time, to start killing people. Laughingly the Don wondered whether he ought to knock the weapon out of the man's hands. It was an achievable enough feat.

'Say your prayers, dwarf,' the assassin hissed dementedly.

Don't bother, the Don felt like adding, prayer feeling like just another of the monumental self-indulgences he had dipped into over the years. God existed but what did it have to do with him? Still, he did not want to appear ungrateful to these men, who had, whatever else they were, lied openly on his behalf, so raising his arm slightly, he flicked the assassin's shooting arm away from Largo's head.

The assassin fired once, the shot travelling straight through the headrest, taking off most of Largo's left ear. The sound of gunfire reminded the Don of the house he had left behind and the people in it. *He* was still alive, but were they? 'My wife,' he stuttered, 'my wife, where is she?' Fired by the sudden return of his senses and his natural patrician indignation, Don Rojo now found himself back in the world of human care again. 'My wife,' he roared. 'What did you do with my wife? I need to get back to her at once, do you hear me? At once!'

'You had better check with our friend first,' shouted the Captain.

'Yes, our friend,' parroted Largo, his loose ear flapping as he spoke, eager that the situation should be resolved without the loss of the other one.

The assassin turned towards the Don open mouthed. Instinctively, his gun turned with him, but not before he had released a second shot, which shattered Largo's arm. The Don, too angry to think of death, grabbed the assassin's gun arm with one hand and his throat with the other, and pinned him to his seat. Acting quickly, the Captain leant over both men and loosened the passenger door to the assassin's left. Using all his strength, he pulled himself, and the other two men who were still struggling with each other, out of the moving car and into a row of newly planted trees.

Josip, who much to his own chagrin had sat with his head in his lap since the shot had been fired, now turned around to close the open door, which was clattering against the car like a broken wing. 'Good, but we need to go back,' he yelled.

'I can't, I really can't,' Largo retorted through clenched teeth. 'I can't use my arm, he shot me.' Balancing himself against the steering wheel, Largo tried to bend it around but the speed of the car, and the slope of the hill, was stronger than the force of his effort. Realising this, Josip pushed open the door and rolled out of his seat and, in seconds, was a ball of speeding dust.

Screaming something indecipherable after him, Largo let the car go its own way as it hurtled farther down the bank and through the gates of a corral into open fields.

The Don looked up. The Captain lay tangled amongst a mesh of young olive trees. He was still moving, but not wholly alert to the fact. A shameful impulse told the Don to feign similar injuries, but who was there to try it on in front of? Like a drunk who has woken up to discover that life will go on, despite the hell of the night before, the Don got up cautiously and started to feel his arms and legs for bruises. There were some but, on the whole, they were not as bad as he had thought – only cosmetic. It was hard to hide his pleasure. You were a little bit hard on yourself back there, he told himself – feeling, if anything, slightly foolish. The finality of the last hour had proved to be a false storm. He had been tested and passed.

Scrambling up from where he had fallen, the assassin, still alive and very angry, pulled his second revolver out of his coat and aimed it at the Don's head. Killing him was pretty much the only thing on his mind now. The gun recoiled slightly as it sent the first of a succession of bullets past the Don's face. The Don did not duck, but instead ran as fast as he could up the path leading back to the road. The assassin, amazed but not disheartened at having missed a target at such close range, reloaded his pistol and, using his left arm as support, squeezed the trigger.

The Don was hit square in the back twice and fell over.

Switching hands, the assassin fired off a third bullet, but as it fell short of its target he felt his back snap with a savage jerk. Before he could turn around he was hit again; this time the blow was not cushioned by shock, and the assassin let out a howl of pain. His back had been struck by lead, not flesh. From up on the bank, Raul Alcazar emptied an entire magazine into the assassin's body before he was satisfied he was dead. Then, dropping his empty revolver, he ran over to where the Don had fallen and knelt down beside him.

'Raul,' the Don croaked, 'it seems as though you've gone and saved my life.'

Alcazar smiled. 'You know, Braulio, I don't think I have.'

The Don returned Alcazar's smile and closed his eyes. His heart was still beating but his breath was faint. Squeezing out a gentle laugh, he whispered quietly, 'I suppose you're offering me a unique opportunity to have my last words recorded for posterity.'

'It's there if you want it.'

'Come on,' the Don croaked, 'you'll be finishing my sentences for me before I even get to the bit about my life flashing before my eyes . . .'

'Harsh, Braulio, that's very harsh.'

The Don laughed, choking lightly, and let himself drift.

It was not that his life was not passing before his eyes, rather that one particular part of it was. Whether this was one memory, or several conflated recollections, he could not tell, but the overall sensation was pure enough to exist for itself. He and his wife were in his observatory listening to music that was asking too much of them, its sound being too grandiose to be contained by life, but too real to exceed it. The music's power and emphasis made them both laugh since the feelings it provoked were almost too passionate to be taken seriously. When the music had ended, his wife had declared that listening to this music was like listening to the Don speak.

'Are you thirsty?'

'No, no thank you.'

Raising his hand in the air, Alcazar waved away

those of his men who had arrived at the scene of the accident. There was, Alcazar thought, no sense in interrupting a dying man's tranquillity.

'Is there anything . . .' Alcazar stopped himself abruptly, shook his head at his reason for stopping, and continued, 'is there anything you would like me to tell your wife and daughters?'

'Are they safe?'

'Yes, I think they are.'

'Well, tell them what you would tell your own daughters,' the Don hissed falteringly and, as if he knew more would be expected of him, added, 'Tell them that I caught up with myself and I was not uncomfortable with what I found . . . that I was given the person I am by God and, despite what you think, Raul, it wasn't for free . . . I've had to pay . . .'

Alcazar raised an eyebrow. Both the Don's eyes were open now and, far from appearing wasted by this final effort, the Don was showing signs of positive reinvigoration. This struck Alcazar as funny and, seeing no reason to hold back, he said so.

Smiling happily, the Don answered, quietly, but very much like a man who had made up his mind to live, 'I'm not sure I'm ready to die yet, I don't know what will happen next . . .'

'No one does, Braulio, not until we've done it. That's what we do everything on the promise of; nothing. Nothing and a small dose of expectation . . .' Smiling, Alcazar reached down to clasp his old friend's shoulder. 'But this small dose, as we both know, it is everything . . .' Alcazar paused. 'Braulio, can you still hear me?'

The Don raised his arm up slightly to signify that he wanted to say something, but allowed it to drop before he got to whatever it was. His eyes closed and his soul careered off into noiseless inconsequence. He was dead.

Back on the track, Alcazar ordered Antonio Mayle's naked body to be cut down from the tree it had been bound to.

'Who thought of mounting him up there like that?' he asked.

No one replied.

'He was always putting people down,' he heard one soldier whisper to another, and there was a grumble of low-level agreement.

'Check if he's still alive. If he is get him to a doctor and if he isn't bury him.'

Turning around slowly, Alcazar began the walk back to the Rojo hacienda. When he got there he would go straight to sleep. He shook his head. Part of him felt as if it would be difficult to take the rest of his life seriously. But part of him would just get on with it.

Over in the bank below, Josip hauled the Captain's twitching body over his shoulder and helped him up on to the road.

'Someone might like to give me a hand,' he called cheerfully. 'I've got him to collect next,' and he pointed to the corral below where Largo's car was cutting giant figures of eight into the freshly ploughed earth.